FU˙ MEMORIES

STEP ASIDE

AND OTHER STORIES

*To Kathryn
from Andrew
x x x*

ANDREW HAIG

Published by Albion Press

ISBN 978-0-9558103-9-8

© Copyright: Andrew Haig
First published December 2015

Printed in Great Britain by
One Digital, Brighton, UK

Future Memories?

I do hope not. There is a distinctly dystopian feel to this collection. Partly this is due to my continuing habit, explicit in my first book *Dreamdays,* of taking my cue from dreams. More to the point though, I feel uneasy about so many things in life, and just where they might be taking us.

Not everything is imagined. *Deliverance*, *High Flyer* and *Midnight Rambler* are uncomfortably close to lived experience. They qualify as future memories only in that I have pushed them another step or two along the road.

I would like to thank my editor partner Jane Edmonds and my poet friend Ted Booth for patiently reading the early drafts and talking some sense into me. Thanks also to Sonal Chaudhary for helping me with the anatomical detail in *Deliverance*, Anne Johnson for helping me with the French in the same story and Helen Joubert for her Photoshop work on the cover.

We were not to know
The white shade lake
Among the cedar trees
Would sometime make
Future memories

The satin cloth night
Also made bid
With warm blown breeze
Leaving scarce hid
Future memories

A child is born
The spiral continues
In ever spun degrees
Soft new sinews and
Future memories

In the house on the road
We were not to guess
Doing as we please
Friends, lovers, the rest
Future memories

The sea at night
A tentative touch
Of intrepid unease
Yielding so much for
Future memories

CONTENTS

STEP ASIDE

"And the winner is…" There followed the traditional agonising pause and the faked fumbling of the envelope. "The winner is…"

At the HKB table, despite the heroic amount of alcohol taken, the theatrical presentation had brought them back to full attention. Tim Harlesden, the creative director and the most senior of the group affected a paternalistic cool but underneath the table his right knee was jigging wildly. Next to him was their guest, the Right Honourable Julia Ormrod, a junior health minister with whom they had worked most closely on the project. It would not have done for him to give way to his excitement in her presence and she, having drunk just mineral water, restricted herself to an indulgent smile as she eyed the rest of their table. Younger (and thirstier), they were on the edge of their seats, scarcely able to bear those remaining seconds. The account executive, the video director and his team, the marketing director and PA from the agency, variously had fists clenched, willing a favourable result, or hands held to mouths or over eyes as though shutting out some horror. Each of them, in those final moments, turned to look at the creative team: Ethan McGuinness, the art director and Sam Ellender, the copywriter.

Ethan was the older of the two – in his late twenties he had already forged a name for himself in the world of commercial advertising. He looked every inch the young creative – hair flopped asymmetrically above Beardslyesque features. Despite the heat inside the auditorium, he wore a silk scarf draped, just so, around his elegant neck. His suit nodded towards the 'formal evening dress' required by their invitations but the waist-length jacket and ultra skinny trousers were made of some iridescent material; his bow tie was a floppy thing in taupe velvet. He made no attempt at decorum and squirmed in his seat with long-fingered hands splayed out towards the stage as if to draw all attention to himself. "Come on, come on," he implored in high-pitched entreaty.

Sam could not have been more different. In his early twenties and just three years out of university, he had made an immediate impact when he joined the agency. He and Ethan had become the creative team charged with government campaigns targeted at the young. Sam had proved himself not only to be a superb copywriter but capable of ideas that reached straight to the hearts of, what, after all, was, his own generation. A serious-minded and acutely intelligent young man, he was confident enough in his abilities not to feel the need to dress the part. He looked more like a city boy: his sandy hair was expensively cut and not for him the designer stubble. The fresh-shaved skin of his handsome face made him look younger even than he was. His dress suit, though bespoke, was utterly conventional. He too showed tension – in his case by leaning forward, his forehead on the table, unable to watch the events on stage.

Tim Harlesden placed a reassuring hand on Sam's shoulder

and allowed his own thoughts to drift back to the first creative meeting.

It had fallen to him to outline the brief:

"We know there is considerable pressure on the health service. It's not the successful ones that are of prime concern. They are cleaned up, registered and dispensed with. All very neat and tidy. Fait-a-complis you might say. It is the unsuccessful that are a disproportionate drain on resources. They have to be helped of course and in a way that involves so many services – ambulance, hospital stays, psychiatric counselling and so on. The unsuccessful are where the problem lies. The figures show – have always shown – that young men between the ages of 20 and 30 are the most inclined to suicide. It is that demographic that we have been asked to address. How, the government is asking, can we make sure that young men are fully informed of the implications of attempted suicide?"

He turned to Sam.

"Sam, why don't we take you as a kind of control? You have your job – not a bad one I'm thinking." A self-congratulatory chuckle went round the table. "And I know that you got married a couple of years ago – Louise isn't it? I met her at the office party last year. Lovely girl and bright too. Doing quite well in public relations if I'm not mistaken. Any children? No, of course not – you are still five years away from the quota threshold. You've got that very tasty flat in Fulham and, if I may say so, a motor I would give my eye teeth for. We all would." Another chuckle travelled round the table.

"In summary: great job, great wife, great flat, great car." He paused before asking what all present knew would be the next big question. "Now here's the thing. What would it take … what would it take for you to reach the point where you would consider … consider even for a moment … taking your own life?"

Sam looked at his colleagues with a shocked look on his face. It wasn't the question. That was something that he considered so hypothetical, so far from any possibility that it scarcely had meaning. The shock derived from being put on the spot. He was an exceptional copywriter who, assigned to a first rate-art director had already in his second year with the agency been cited for a D&AD award. Now he was not just expected to make some intelligent insights into the thinking of young men but he was the very subject of research. This seemed too personal. He didn't want to go there.

"I … I don't know. It is so difficult to imagine circumstances where … It wouldn't be the job. If I got made redundant, well, I think with my track record I could find another … I get offers all the time." He had intended this as a tension lightener, but looking at the stony expressions on the faces of his seniors moved swiftly on. "No, a job wouldn't do it, nor the material loss that might go hand-in-hand. Losing the flat, the car – it's true I enjoy my life style but when all is said and done, these are just things and things can be acquired again." He gulped – he was required to expand further and the thoughts were becoming more painful.

"My marriage? How would I feel if that fell apart. Well … obviously I'd be shattered but even then, I doubt it would be enough. Again, there are always other opportunities … " He gave a weak smile matched by a few sympathetic responses from around the table.

"Serious illness? I'm not even sure about that. My own father died of emphysema. The strange thing is that it was the making of him. He had been a quick-tempered and arrogant sort of guy. Something about the illness changed him. He became very introspective and calm. It's not an exaggeration to say that we had all been slightly afraid of him – even my mother. But we grew to like the new him – love him even. He died a man at peace with himself."

The table had fallen silent and Sam realised that he was rambling. So … what? What could possibly take him to the brink of suicide? It came to him.

"My child. If serious harm came to my child – abduction, murder, death in an accident – that kind of thing. I shouldn't be able to bear that. Sure, I haven't got one yet – the threshold and all that – but I can't imagine anything worse. Unlike things or even relationships, the authorities would never allow a replacement, even in those circumstances."

At this he fell into silence. This hadn't been the kind of day that he'd envisaged. These weren't the kind of thoughts he was accustomed to.

But Sam was first choice for the agency. His anti-smoking campaign had been a sensation. Of course the video direction had been fabulous and the song that carried the narrative had become a hit in its own right, but the concept had been his and his alone.

The melody was beautiful. In a minor key, it was played to a plaintive acoustic accompaniment with a ghostly choral backing which started at a barely audible whisper and grew to a keening lament at the last.

At eight I showed her all my toys
We played the livelong day
My special friend
My special friend
Together come what may

At ten I showed her all my books
Our favourite Pooh the bear
We read and laughed
And laughed and read
We loved them then and there

At twelve I showed her how to kiss
And we walked hand in hand
The boys they mocked
The girls they talked
But we just found it grand

And then I showed her cigarettes
And how to smoke them cool
A grown-up game
A grown-up game
Behind the sheds at school

When we left, we had our fun
At pub and club and show
We laughed and danced
And drank our fill
And smoked 'til time to go

And then I showed a wedding ring
We vowed 'til death do part
Now death has come
My love is gone
There's aching in my heart

I wish I'd known what I now know
The death that stalks our fun
I'd give just love
And not the smoke
That took my only one.

The video had been in soft focus black and white, filmed for the early verses in wistful nostalgic style. Really beautifully filmed and edited. The childhood scenes segued into elegantly shot cigarette smoke for the middle section, then transposed to swirling mist in the later funeral scenes. No medical facts, no gruesome shots of diseased lungs – just a sad sad story that everyone could relate to. The ad was seen not just in its broadcast slots in cinemas and on TV but was viewed millions of times online. The song held the number one slot for fifteen weeks. That would have meant nothing had it been ineffective but the opposite was true. Cigarette sales slumped by a massive 16% in the first month alone and remained firm at an 11% reduction almost a year later.

Such was its success that the government had commissioned a copycat campaign, but this time addressing itself to the problem of binge drinking. Nobody thought that the trick would work a second time but how wrong they were. Pub, club and supermarket sales slumped and the revised song climbed once more into the charts.

Freedom of choice to smoke and drink at will (and there were plenty of voices calling for such freedom) was one thing, the growing demand on health service resources, quite another. It was too early to tell if the anti-smoking success would lead to the anticipated reduction in cancers and other health consequences, but research implied that the benefits would be significant within the following five years. What gave hope was the success of the anti-drinking campaign, where some of the results were more immediately evident. Within two months, the flood of casualties to A&E of a Saturday night had dropped by a third; incidents of violent disorder had dropped by much the same proportion.

Encouraged by this, the Government had embarked on its latest campaign, again aimed at relieving the strain on resources. With the population approaching 75 million, and living longer at that, it was clear that the welfare state would become untenable without further changes in social attitudes.

The one couple, one child policy had been in place for five years but had proved horrendously difficult to administer in a state that still considered itself to be a liberal democracy. Immigration had been practically halted for the best part of a decade but still the population seemed to creep upwards and so did the demand for health and welfare resources. The government had turned its attention to the incidence of suicide.

HKB Advertising was now the 'go to' agency given the success of the smoking and drinking campaigns. Sam and his art director were the 'go to' team. The Government had sidestepped its own procedures, which required competitive pitching, and had made a direct commission. The pressure on

Sam was enormous.

He had six months not just to come up with the concept and the script but, with Ethan, to supervise the shoot and edits for various media outlets. Conscientious as ever, he extended his working days to upwards of fifteen hours.

He began with extensive research that included surveys among the young, health professionals and social workers, and read everything he could on the subject. He then made pitch after pitch to his superiors in the agency before they settled on a version that they were able to pitch in turn to the ministry. Only then was he ready to brief the video team.

Ironically, given the discussion at the first meeting, the quality of his life outside of work began to deteriorate markedly. He and Louise had prided themselves on balance in their relationship. Both were successful in their careers and both accepted that the routine and the chores of domestic life should be shared. They were young, attractive and gregarious, with many friends with whom they had, hitherto, shared a busy social life.

Now Sam, obsessed by his commission and increasingly exhausted, began to neglect his side of the bargain. At first Louise tolerated his withdrawal from shopping, cooking and cleaning on the understanding that things would return to normal on completion of the project. His unwillingness to meet or entertain friends, to go to the cinema, the theatre or the gigs they both loved, she took less well, but made the best of it by making a social life of her own.

Inevitably the situation impacted on their sexual life. If he was often too tired – all energy expended at work – she was ceasing to find him attractive. He looked increasingly haunted

– pale and haggard, often unshaven and wearing yesterday's clothes. She would catch whiffs of body odour as he came to bed and had no desire to draw closer. He had been an attentive and empathetic partner but he no longer so much as asked her how her day had been and responded to her enquiries about his with non-committal shrugs.

Returning from the office late one night and distracted by thoughts of what was still to be done, he ploughed their beloved Porsche into the back of a van waiting at a red light. It was an indication of how much their lives had changed that both he and Louise accepted the accident with resigned indifference. It seemed somehow another inevitability in the new way of things.

Louise had started to stay out later with her friends and occasionally she had not returned until morning. Although Sam had been momentarily concerned about this, his attention was soon reclaimed by problems with the shoot. With weeks to go before completion though, he was devastated by Louise's announcement of her pregnancy. In compliance with the quota and their even-handed approach to the relationship, he had taken full responsibility for their contraception, but even that he appeared to have neglected on one of their increasingly rare sexual encounters.

For a moment he was jolted into concerns other than those posed by work. He had looked forward to the time when they would be permitted to have a child, but he knew too well the penalty for pregnancy outside of the programme. While the Government stopped short of insistence on termination, the child and the parents faced a future without any benefit or support from the state beyond a rudimentary education at special and deliberately inferior schools. Sam immediately applied his thoughts to how they might outmanoeuvre the system – they knew of others who had found a way – but Louise was not prepared to take the risk with her career or a future child's prospects. She arranged, without compunction, for the abortion.

Sam now withdrew still further into himself, unwilling or unable to talk about his disappointment and anger. Louise grew tired of trying to explain herself and one night he returned to their now dishevelled flat to find a note on the mantelpiece and she gone. Even his distress at this catastrophe seemed short-lived. He threw himself with renewed intensity into the final editing and scheduling of the campaign.

Once again the ads created an extraordinary swell of comment and controversy. Once again the music gained a momentum of its own. Once again response from the target audience proved what an effective and valuable communicator Sam was.

"The contenders are ... "

There were four finalists in the Social Campaign category. All of them had been broadcast on all the relevant media and were well-known by those present. They were shown again here as part of the build-up to the award.

First was the campaign created for Oxfam by the much-in-demand E-Agency – the E standing for both Electronic and Ethical. It was a highly professional piece, drawing attention to the refugee crisis caused by the catastrophic sea level rises in Bangladesh and the Philippines. The cutting back and forth between scenes of the Thames flooding in the UK and damage in Asia was original and effective in so far as it attempted to use our own relatively minor tragedies as a springboard for imagining situations a hundred times worse. Unfortunately, the scenes in the latter part, of hollow-faced and starving children clinging to mothers carrying them through the floods, were reminiscent of many other such appeals.

Second was a recruitment campaign commissioned by the Humanist Society. It was the work of a mainstream agency, Lagano Forbes, whose CEO was an outspoken secularist. He had offered the agency's services for free. In truth it had proved extremely contentious, being a compilation of harrowing scenes of conflict and oppression, of death and destruction. Rough textured lettering was stamped over each ghastly sequence, identifying the key protagonists: SUNNIS, PROTESTANTS, CATHOLICS, JEWS, BUDDHISTS, SIKHS, SHIAS, HINDUS and so on. Each stamping was accompanied by ear-splitting discordant choral snatches from Penderecki's Auschwitz Oratorium. Gradually the cacophony and grim scenes faded to be replaced by a pastoral setting with the sound only of bird song. The website address of the Humanist Society was superimposed. The implication was clear and the piece was undeniably powerful but its broadcast had been met by angry protests outside the agency from various religious groups. Certainly it was considered to be a brave and provocative move by D&AD to feature it among the nominations.

The third piece for SUSTRANS provided a much-needed

dose of humour. It began as a paean to the motorcar. The agency had gone to the trouble of building a sleek-bodied high-performance saloon that was shown in every possible clichéd situation – racing along Alpine hairpins, shot from above as it travelled at impossible speed through miraculously emptied city streets. There were constant cuts to sexy details of bodywork of both car and glamorous passengers – he driving of course and she casting lustfully admiring glances as she closed her hands over his which, in turn, were caressing the gear stick.

The car passed from left to right across the screen. Then out of view, there was the screech of heavy braking. The camera panned round and located the car, which was now caught in an almighty traffic jam. This was followed by a close up of the now red-faced and angry couple pounding on the horn. A family cycling along the adjacent cycle lane stopped, looked in the open window and asked if the occupants were OK. "Push off," was the reply – and the cycling family did just that smiling happily to themselves. The camera climbed up high above the endless car jam, alongside which groups of happy cyclists glided past. The camera pulled up to a beautiful summer sky. "Push off" read the final caption.

And then, at last, it was the turn of HKB's 'Step Aside' for HM Government.

It began with the heart-breaking melody and poignant lyrics that had become such a signature of Sam's work, as was the seductive camera work and the message delivered through a series of emotional metaphors rather than dry facts and figures.

The piece began with a child walking high on a sunlit mountain path. As the child climbed, a whispered song began like a voice on the wind.

Here, here you are
Climbing now up and up
To where you're born to be
Towards the sun
To the peak
And then you will be free

As the camera cut away and then back to the climbing figure, the viewer saw each time that the child had aged from toddler to young boy, from young boy to teenager, then to young man.

Before this process continued they saw something else. Behind the figure on the narrow path were other figures, both male and female. The camera panned down the line of climbers, jostling to get past the lead figure. They regressed in age as the camera descended.

Here, here they are
Firm, strong, young and proud
Climbing the future to see
Theirs to have
Yours to give
And then you will be free

The camera returned to the lead climber. He was still a young man but he was struggling to make headway. Unshaven and breathing heavily, he stumbled from time to time. And then, quite suddenly he ran to the edge of the path and leapt over the edge. Instead of plummeting he took flight like a mountain eagle. From below the camera followed him silhouetted against the sun. As the chorus swelled (… and then you will be free), the camera was now above the gliding bird, wings outstretched, and below was the joyful stream of youngsters now making their way up the unblocked path.

Then came the voiceover: a soothing, confiding male voice – one recognisably that of a popular actor:

You've tried, we know you have, and well done for that. But let's face it, you have no work or at least not work you enjoy or that pays much. You don't own your home or maybe you sleep rough. What does that do to your relationships? What does it say about you? There are others now behind you, ready to give life a try. Would you stand in their way? Deny them the chance? Why not step aside and let others through? We can help you to do this in a way that is painless and peaceful and, what's more, we will set you free.

Again the chorus swelled and the young man dressed in clean white clothes was shown with a young woman on his arm wandering through a meadow suffused with sunlight.

I stepped to one side
And let the others through
They passed singing by me
The gift was mine
A life not lived
And now I'm free, I'm free

The couple walked towards the light as the song faded and the voice-over came in once more:

> Call 0800 702702 and talk to a step aside counsellor who will help you make your choice. Or visit stepaside.gov.uk for more information. £1000 will be paid to a recipient of your choice if you step aside with us.

The last scene was, again, shot from a height with birds wheeling in the sky and the couple far below walking hand in hand through the flowered meadow. The freedom song faded with the image

There was a stunned silence lasting for maybe five whole seconds. Then as the lights were brought up the cheering and applause began with many of the guests standing to show their appreciation, some dabbing their eyes as they did so.

"…and the winner is…"

During the pausing and envelope fumbling Ethan looked round to his colleague to see how he was coping with the tension. He wasn't. Sam had let his head sink down to the table – his hands either side. Ethan put a reassuring arm round his shoulders and, smiling indulgently, leant down to whisper in his ear:

"Come on old son, we're nearly there – this is our night. Hope you've got a speech ready. Poor show for a star copywriter if you haven't." Chuckling at his own joke he turned his attention back to the stage.

"…HKB Advertising for 'Step aside'."

The room erupted in a riot of whoops, cheers and applause. The entire HKB team had risen to their feet and were embracing each other in congratulation. All except Sam who remained where he sat, head forward on the table. Ethan prodded him:

"Come on Sam, move your arse. Let's get up there."

But Sam was going nowhere. He stayed still, very still. The hubbub in the room gradually subsided as the audience, wearying of their own hand-clapping, began wondering why the winning team had not appeared on stage. Eyes turned to the HKB table where Ethan could be seen shaking his partner's shoulder. Was he drunk? Poor kid, the excitement of the night must have been too much for him. Complete silence had now fallen.

Ethan went to grab one of Sam's hands to try and pull him to his feet but stopped short at the sight of the empty pill bottle held in his grip.

DELIVERANCE

… the overall length shall be a minimum of 260cm, and a maximum of 270cm… the distance from the tip to the centre of gravity shall be a minimum of 90cm and a maximum of 110cm… the diameter of the shaft at the thickest point shall be a minimum of 25mm and a maximum of 30mm… the width of the cord grip shall be a minimum of 15cm and a maximum of 16cm… the cross-section shall be regularly circular throughout… from the grip the javelin shall taper gradually to the front and rear tips.

Alan would have preferred a smoother path on such a steep descent, letting gravity gently have its way – the hard work done. But this was no such path. It was narrow and winding with a gulley cutting down its centre, gouged, he imagined, by spring melt waters. The way was littered with rocks and boulders that would have been flushed down the hillside over time. This meant stepping deeply from one level to the next, his tired legs taking the shock. After hop-skipping down for 40 minutes and feeling increasingly weary, he decided to look for a stave to take his weight. The woods he was passing through were primarily of oak, and the fallen branches scattered around looked unlikely to serve the purpose. They were rough to the touch, covered as they were with nubby bark and lichen. Nevertheless, he selected one of about the right length and stripped it of superfluous side branches. It lasted barely a minute before, as he placed his full weight on it at a deep step-down, it shattered in three places. He fell forward and would have pitched face down onto the rocks had he not been able to steady himself by grabbing hold of the branch of another tree growing by the side of the path.

He stayed still for a minute until his heart quietened and his breathing settled. What, he thought, did one actually do in an emergency – say he'd fallen and broken his leg? Foolishly he'd left his mobile back at the house and anyway, his navigation had been approximate. He would have had great difficulty explaining exactly where he was. Annie and the kids would have raised the alarm after his failure to appear but, again, he had been less than specific about his route for the day – it was his freedom jaunt after all! In a way the thought thrilled him. He'd got away with the tumble but had he not, he was confident that the ingenuity he prided himself on would have gotten him through. 'There is always a solution,' he was fond of saying. Still, what would he have done?

As he was mulling over this hypothetical problem, he found himself absent-mindedly running his hands over the bark of the tree that had arrested his fall. Smooth beige leatherette surface with few imperfections – it was an ash, not uncommon among the oaks. The piece he had held onto was no more than a sapling growing straight and true. On an impulse he reached into his daypack and pulled out his Swiss Army knife, selecting the miniature saw. It took a while but hacking at the base of the sapling he eventually managed to wrench it free.

There were very few side growths to cut away and the final stave stood a couple of feet higher than himself. Rather than cut it back to waist height he decided on a more rustic look – that of a herdsman – and accepted it as it was.

This worked well on the rest of his descent: instead of letting his weight fall onto the stick, he was able effectively to climb down the longer pole, having planted it firmly at a lower level. Filled with sap, it bowed and sprang in a way that took all of the jolting from his movements and showed no sign of shattering as had the dry and brittle oak.

Later, pleasantly tired by his day, he sat with his wife Annie and the twins Rose and Nick on the veranda of their gîte, sipping a glass of wine and hoping that they could enjoy the moment without interruption from Deliverance Boy.

He it was who had ghosted into their lives on the day of their arrival. As they began to unpack the car, an arm had sort of insinuated itself into their huddle around the boot. They had turned to look at its owner. He was a strange-looking lad, quite short and scrawny, obviously young. Alan thought he was no more than 14. He had the face of an adult though, with eyes of the palest blue, giving him an almost sightless look. His unruly hair stuck up like clumps of straw. He was dressed in battered denim dungarees with a dirty torn T-shirt beneath. On his feet was a primitive pair of sandals made, as far as they could see, from old tyre rubber. He was offering to help move their bags into the converted barn that was to be their home for the next two weeks.

"No that's OK we can man…" The boy didn't budge.

"Oh…er…nous n'avons pas besoin d'aide," said Alan

dredging up his French. He smiled at the boy as he spoke.

His face impassive, the lad thrust his arms several times towards the bags. The meaning was clear – he was *insisting* on helping. They gave way and allowed him to carry the bulk of their luggage into the building. This he did without once speaking or changing his expression.

When they had finished, Alan felt in his pocket and with characteristic English embarrassment fished out a ten-euro note and waved it tentatively at the boy, who, giving a half smile – almost disdainful Alan thought – sauntered off down the path without taking the money.

Later as they ate their supper they had discussed the strange boy. It was Rose who finally made the connection. A few months previously they had, as a family, watched the movie *Deliverance* on TV.

"Remember the boy on the bridge. He was a hillbilly kid or somethin'. There was somethin' weird about him. Don't you remember? He played the banjo and that fat guy like challenged him to a musical duel. God he was well spooky that Deliverance Boy."

Deliverance Boy he became.

That first evening was fine. Having spent much of the day travelling, they were happy to explore their immediate surroundings before chilling on the veranda as the sun began to set. They congratulated themselves on having gone with a rental company that specialised in properties which were out of the mainstream; in their case a working farm in Haute Provence. Their hearts had lifted on arrival, the entrance to the property being a honey-bricked archway topped by a chateau-style turret. Once they had passed through, they continued on a dusty path through an olive grove and to their barn, glowing gold in the late sun, grape vines tethered against its walls. The upper floor was where they were to live. This was reached by a wide stone stairway. The ground floor had been unchanged from its original purpose as a hay barn and store. They presumed animals had been quartered there in the winter, giving warmth to those above. Along the length of the building reached by the stairs was a generous balcony shaded by yet more vines.

Before unpacking they had clambered up the stairs and gazed out at their surroundings. Directly opposite was another barn, clearly still in use. It must be a sawmill thought Alan. There was a huge pile of fresh-cut logs in front of it and glimpses of metal machinery behind. Hmm, could be noisy, he thought, but on the other hand this is what they had signed up for. Living on a working farm for two weeks would be an education for the children and, anyway, they would be elsewhere during the day.

In the distance, to their right, they could see the farmhouse and beyond that the lower hills giving way to Alpine mountains silhouetted a delicate blue on the skyline.

Their unpacking done and a pasta simmering on the stove, they sat out on the veranda luxuriating in the evening sun. The adults sipped at their first glass of wine, while the children, comfortable in their new surroundings, curled up in their basket chairs and texted their friends.

The second day was when their problems began. They had looked forward to another evening on the veranda after a busy day exploring the neighbourhood. Showered and relaxed, they sat watching the sunset as they had the night before.

BOOM. The explosion was loud enough to cause each of them to duck. BOOM. Another one. For a moment Alan forgot himself:

"What the fuck!" He looked in the direction that the sound appeared to have come from. There was a puff of rapidly dissipating smoke above the woodshed. Below it and poking over the pile of logs, he spotted a length of metal tube. A country boy himself, he knew what it was – a bird scarer. But why now? Why here? As he looked, the tell-tale thatch of unruly hair appeared above the logs and the barrel was angled towards them. BOOM. The kid was attacking them! There was no doubt that they were his target.

"Oi!" yelled Alan "Stop that – fuck off!" Remembering that the boy spoke no English, his tirade continued with a stream of roughly appropriate franglais:

"Arrêter now! Sors d'ici, idiot!" He instantly regretted the last word, suspecting the boy might well be. BOOM. A final shot was aimed in their direction and then the head and the tube disappeared from view.

He turned to look at Annie and the children who sat frozen in what? Fear, disbelief? There was a moment's silence.

"Dad, you swore," said Nick.

"I'm sorry," said Alan. "It's just a bird scarer. It makes a hell of a noise but it won't harm us. What on earth does the kid think he's doing? Maybe it's a bizarre sort of welcome."

They had no more trouble that night and were able to settle into a pleasant enough evening. Hopefully the boy had worked through whatever was going on in his head and surely by now his own parents would have remonstrated with him?

The attack on the third evening disabused them of any such hope. It continued on and off for the best part of an hour. After each explosion Alan yelled with mounting fury at their assailant, remembering at last some choice expletives:

"Petit salaud! Espèce de con! Emmerdeur! Imbécile! Any sensitivity concerning the 'I' word had long since evaporated. It would go quiet for a while and just when he thought their torment was over – BOOM!

Annie had gone inside soon after the start of the onslaught, slamming the door angrily behind her. The children stayed for a while, open-mouthed with incredulity at the sight of a kid not much older than themselves getting away with such outrageous behaviour. Soon though their attention returned to their phones and they drifted off to join their mother.

On the fourth evening it began again at much the same time, just as they came out to relax on the veranda to make the most of the late sun. Alan yelled and screamed at the boy as the explosions rang out, but after half an hour and with no sign of abatement, he snapped. Without knowing what he intended to do, he clattered down the steps and ran full pelt towards the log pile, screaming out every piece of abuse that came to mind. He thought later that it was just as well he hadn't come face-to-face with Deliverance Boy. What would he have done? As it happened the kid had turned and run along the path back to the farmhouse taking his weapon with him. As he ran he emitted a high-pitched cackling laugh. This was fun for him.

Made anxious by the turn of events, on the fifth day Alan had negotiated the long day's walk during which he had picked up the stave. He had needed time on his own, away from family responsibility and away from the boy and the farm. It had taken several hours and some fierce walking to quieten the anger raging within him, not to mention the shame of his own ineffectuality. He had stomped up the first slopes of the day with wild murderous fantasies blighting his enjoyment: imagining turning a corner, encountering Deliverance Boy and doing god knows what to him. Later, the heat and increasingly fabulous views as he climbed higher settled him and he regained his customary sense of calm.

Annie and the children had spent their day swimming in a local river and picnicking on its banks. They were feeling equally relaxed.

As he told them of his day, he kept looking compulsively to the door against which he had propped his stave. At first he couldn't think why he should admire it so. It reminded him of when he had spent an obscene amount of money on his road bike. How, as it stood in their hallway at home, he had felt a compulsion to go and view it every half hour or so – it really was a beauty. But what was this? – just a stick when all was said and done But there was something familiar in its shape and feel. And then he remembered.

Never a great sportsman at school, he had discovered, nevertheless, that he had an aptitude for the javelin and (not that there had been much competition) he competed in that discipline in athletics meetings against other schools. He had become quite good and, as far as he knew, retained the county record for his then age group. A javelin thrower gets to know everything there is to know about his missile – its dimensions, weight, centre of gravity and so on, not to mention its ideal trajectory. His stave seemed already, at a glance, to conform to many of these attributes. He tried to talk to Rose and Nick about this but they had heard his reminiscences about his athletic prowess one too many times and their attention soon turned back to the games on their phones.

Annie was talking to him about the children's swimming progress and what they might do as a family the next day

"…I thought if we stopped off for supplies at the market in Banon, we could…Alan are you listening to me?"

He wasn't. His eyes had slid over again to the stave and his mind was elsewhere. Just as he was about to perjure himself by claiming to be paying full attention, the first of the evening's explosions rang out. Deliverance Boy had embarked on his evening mission to lay siege to the interlopers. The children barely looked up from their phones but their mother had turned angrily on her heels

"Oh for Christ's sake! I'm going in to start the supper."

Alan turned his gaze to the barn and the woodpile over the top of which he could just see the boy's head bobbing up and down. For a moment he considered whether to re-enact his strategy of the night before – and run straight at the little sod. It had worked then after all. Annie disappeared through the door and slammed it forcefully behind her. He turned at the sound and saw his stave about to topple, shaken from its perch. He moved quickly, catching it by the middle and marvelled again at how beautifully balanced it felt.

His daypack was still where he had thrown it on his return and he fished out his knife, this time opening out the large blade. He set to, scraping away the papery bark and cutting out the occasional imperfection. It was a remarkably blemish-free piece of wood with, crucially, no knots along its length. The task was soon accomplished.

"What are you doing dad?" asked Nick, and Alan smiled to himself at the fact that this simple, primitive activity had been enough, for however short a time, to distract his son from his phone. He thought it best not to reply but to continue to intrigue the boy by bending to his task.

Next: find the point of balance and, therefore, the centre of gravity by balancing it on one finger.

"Can I try that dad?"asked Rose, and he let her, while saying nothing.

Now it was the turn of the rasp attachment as he attended to one end. He remembered that he needed to create a conical gradation for optimal strength, and he set to work, turning the rod frequently to ensure centrality. Both children wanted a go and he agreed with a warm feeling he hadn't experienced much in recent times, of bonding satisfyingly with them.

"Once we've carved the cone," he said, "we take the last inch to a really sharp point. If it's too long, it will snap on impact."

"Dinner's ready," called Annie and, hungry now, they abandoned the task for the night. It occurred to Alan, as he took a final look over to the woodpile, that they had spent the best part of an hour getting this far and had scarcely been aware of their assailant. The boy must have become bored with the lack of reaction and shuffled off home.

"Annie, keep my dinner warm can you, I'll be back in a mo." Alan had decided to do something he should have done when their problems with the boy first started. He followed him down to the farmhouse and rapped on the door. The boy opened it with the insolent little grin he had treated them to on the day they arrived.

"Ou sont ton père et ta mère?" Alan demanded.

The boy stood aside to reveal his parents sitting at a table behind him. They were at supper. They gazed impassively at Alan, chewing meanwhile and waiting for him to say something.

"I want to complain about…" The boy's father shrugged with exaggerated indifference.

"Je ne parle pas Anglais," he muttered and returned his attention to his plate. Bugger, thought Alan, and wished he had rehearsed his French beforehand.

"Nous…nous ne sommes pas hereux…" Again the indifferent shrug. Alan battled on:

"Votre fils…tout les soires…il nous a attaqué avec les explosifs." The farmer looked up with the same washed out expressionless eyes that his son too possessed.

"Des explosifs?" he queried wearily.

"Oui," responded Alan, "pour effrayer les oiseaux…tout les soirs…Boom, boom, boom." The man gave a condescending smile – and after a long pause, spoke as if to an idiot.

"Monsieur, c'est une ferme. Comprenez vous? Une ferme!"

"Yes I know…I mean je comprends," stuttered Alan feeling unnerved. The whole family stared at him as though he was some holy fool. "Mais…" but the man cut in.

"Les fermes sont des endroits bruyants. Les animaux – meuh, meuh. Les machines – les tracteurs, les scies, et oui, les explosifs pour effrayer les oiseaux," he sneered, clearly mocking his guest.

"Mais, merci, pas pendant la soirée. Votre fils et un délinquent…" He again regretted his choice of word – it was the only one he could think of on the spur of the moment.

The sarcastic smiles faded from the three faces confronting him and the man rose abruptly and threateningly to his feet. Now he raised his voice and emphasising each word repeated, "LES... FERMES... SONT... DES... ENDROITS... BRUYANTS. BONSOIR MONSIEUR." Alan backed through the door and as it was shut firmly behind him he was sure he could hear a chorus of cackles. He regained the path feeling thoroughly defeated. What, he thought, would he say to Annie?

In fact his report was neutral. He had remonstrated with the parents and hoped that that would be the end of the matter. Please let it be so, he thought to himself, without, it must be said, much expectation.

The next day was a full one. They visited the local market which, much to their parents' surprise, charmed the children much as it did them with its sights and smells and sheer authenticity. They then treated themselves to a terrific lunch at an outdoor café in the main square before an afternoon of kayaking.

They returned to the gîte as tired and content as they had been all holiday and, after a shower each, they settled on the veranda with cold drinks and huge slices of pizza that they had bought earlier at the market. They knew full well that no one would be up to cooking after such a day.

Five minutes was all they had before the first explosion of the evening. There he was, peering above his parapet, his 'shotgun' pointed their way. Annie's reaction was as abrupt as it had been the preceding evening.

"Your talk worked well then," she said. "I'm eating inside." And she stalked off. The kids watched with a sort of dazed fascination as Deliverance Boy let loose with another. It failed, however, to interrupt their greedy pizza slurping.

Alan felt, as before, a flood of anger that this appalling boy should be allowed to disrupt their holiday in this way, and frustration at his inability to do anything about it. But he remembered how the activity of the previous night had distracted all of them from the outrage. Pushing the last of his pizza into his mouth, he reached for the stave.

"Are we sharpening the point now dad?" asked Rose.

"We certainly are," he said, "I'll do that. It shouldn't take long and then you can help me with the rest. For starters can you look around in the barn and see if you can find any string?" The children went off in high spirits and within a few minutes he had whittled the end of the stave to the sharpest of points right in the radial centre – perfect!

"Look what we found dad," said Nick. "It was hanging on a nail." He handed over a coil of twine.

"Well done you two, that's exactly what we need. But first there's something else for you to do." The previous night he had marked the centre of gravity and now he produced some sheets of rough sandpaper and some sanding blocks that he had picked up from a stall in the market. "Put the javelin flat on the table there and you can take an end each. We need to sand down from the middle to the tips so that they gently taper. It will reduce the weight but also improve the aerodynamics so it flies well through the air."

The children amazed him, working with concentration and energy. He reminded them to keep turning the javelin at frequent intervals to keep the tapering centred along the length. Apart from providing the occasional bit of muscle to deal with a recalcitrant bump, he left the children to complete the task. Within the hour, there it was – a javelin if ever there was one.

"Can we throw it now dad?" said Rose.

"Two things to do first," he replied. "Because we've shaved away some of the thickness, we have to find the centre of gravity again. Here, Rose, you know what to do."

His daughter moved her hand along the stave, finding once again the exact point of balance, which was duly marked.

"The next thing *I* should do," said their father. "It's a bit tricky." He measured a regulation eight centimetres either side of the centre mark and, making a loop of the twine along the length, began to bind carefully over it with tightly drawn, even loops. When he'd covered the distance between the marks, he fed the end of the twine through the protruding loop and drew it through to complete the job.

"Now", he said, "we're ready to throw."

They descended the steps from the porch onto the grassy area below and the children watched in fascination as he made his preparations. Holding the javelin by the cord handle, above his right shoulder, elbow bent, he flexed it in the evening breeze. It was perfectly balanced and weighted, bouncing in his hand as if anxious to be released. Each upward movement made it weightless. Down, it was heavy as clay. Whuh was the sound it made with each bounce. Whuh... whuh...whuh.

... to hold the javelin properly, you have to place it in the fold of your hand, with your palm up, so that it's in line with the direction

that you'll be throwing in. It has to lie along the length of your palm instead of across from it… throw the javelin when your arm is up as high as possible… the javelin release angle should account for aerodynamic lift and drag… experts recommend 33 degrees as the optimum angle.

He was amazed at how it all came back to him: the run up, the release, the recovery. Although his arms were unused to throwing, they were fresh, and he delighted himself with his first throw.

… the javelin's trajectory during its flight will hopefully follow the path of an arc but because the javelin is straight and unbending the javelin will tangent the arc, and the airflow that meets it will alter during its entire flight… the angle of incidence is the angle of the javelin to this airflow… this angle determines the lift and drag of the javelin and will alter with varying wind conditions, hence a low release angle into a headwind will give lift.

It was perfect. It rose thrumming into the evening sky, not so steeply that its own weight pulled it back on itself but arcing gracefully up, and then, at the highest point, appearing to hang horizontally for a moment, before the tip was reluctantly pulled down and back to earth. Thwud. It hit the ground at a perfect angle, burying itself decisively in the grass. A 15-metre throw minimum. Rose and Nick stood open-mouthed as the wanging sound of the still vibrating javelin faded in the silence of the glade.

The first week of the holiday had been a little unsatisfactory for Alan. Leaving aside the antics of Deliverance Boy, he realised that it was always Annie who organised the family's entertainment. the children, quite understandably, looking to her for their enjoyment. And when not swimming or kayaking, they seemed otherwise unable to take their eyes off their phones, either endlessly texting their friends or playing asinine games. Other than the day at the market, any attempt at serious sight-seeing had bored them and he had given up trying to engage them in such things.

Now there was this. Javelin throwing became the main focus of each evening. He taught Nick and Rose everything he knew about the art. How to build up speed with the body turning sideways to the direction of throw; how to relax the arm held loosely above the shoulder; how to lean back and extend the throwing arm behind in the moment before release; how to throw at the perfect angle; how to follow through and recover balance.

They improved rapidly and, fortunately, at much the same rate. Day after day they threw, beating each other alternately by small increments until the record was set at a distance that even he had difficulty reaching, although he made a point of falling just short, so thrilled was he by the children's concentration and absorption.

The pyrotechnics continued most evenings but subsided more quickly, and several times Alan spotted the boy standing upright and peering at them with what appeared to be intense curiosity. He even wondered whether he should call him over and invite him to have a go, but a fresh explosion was enough to renew his animosity.

If anything, he worried about Annie. He was concerned that his gain with the children she might feel as her loss. Although they didn't really talk about it; the focus, the highlight of the day, had become the evening competition.

The last few days of their stay followed much the same pattern. They went out early, especially on days when the sawmill was in operation. The children had settled into a routine of swimming or kayaking and their parents, having given up the attempt to introduce a note of culture, were content to sun themselves by the river, books in hand, while they kept an eye on them. In many ways it was the best part of the day for the family as a whole .

Annie had taken to disappearing inside as soon as they returned to the farm. While she prepared the evening meal, she turned the CD player up loud, to drown out the sound of the nightly bombardment. And bombarded they were at the same time on each of their remaining nights. It had ceased to bother Alan and the children – they were far too concentrated on the latest throw record. During the final evening it was broken in turn by Nick and then Rose, and was now fully five metres further on from where they had started.

On their last morning they were up early to load the car, anxious to leave before the sawmill started up. Although the thought was unspoken, it was as though each wanted to leave the farm at its peaceful best.

The children and Annie strapped themselves into their seats while Alan cast a final look around at the undeniably beautiful setting which had nevertheless been tarnished by the daily attacks. Of Deliverance Boy he could see no sign, but from the deep shade of the woodshed a pair of pale blue eyes followed their every move.

"Come on Alan," urged Annie. "We need to make a move if

we're going to make that ferry tomorrow."

"OK love," he replied. But there was one more thing he needed to do.

The javelin stood leaning against the side of the car. He had sharpened it to a fresh point for their final throw the night before. As usual he had held his throw back then so as not to eclipse the children's efforts. Now, though, he was free to let rip. One last full-out attempt.

"Come on Alan. Let's go."

"OK, I'm there." He picked up the stave, cradled it back in his hand above his shoulder, felt again the weight/no weight bouncing and the gentle whuh whuh sound as it faced into the breeze. He took a short run-up, turned sideways to his target, pulled back his throwing arm and, hooking his finger behind the cord to create some spin, released a mighty throw.

The javelin described a perfect arc up into the blue sky. As he recovered his balance, he watched it level at the highest point and marvelled again at it seeming to hang motionless before the tip began to drop. And then, suddenly, he didn't want to see any more. It was perfect at that moment. Turning on his heel he loped back to the car, jumped into the driver's seat, fired the ignition and, without a backward glance, drove towards the arch and out onto the open road.

… the pitching moment is the term given to describe the actual moment in flight when the javelin starts to tip over for its descent due to the effect of the airflow hitting the shaft of the javelin …

Facing into the sun, the ice-blue eyes at first saw nothing, although their owner heard a faint whuh whuh sound. From out of the glare, an object froze for a moment high above him. Then it accelerated rapidly as it skittered down from the sky.

Deliverance Boy did not move. Why would he? In the second or so available, any move could just as well put him in the line of fire. Best stand still and take your chances.

The fibres of a shirt, encountered first by a sharpened tip thrown with force, will present little obstacle, parting easily to permit access to the skin.

Human skin has several functions, including armouring the body against such intrusion, but will be unlikely to fare better than the cloth. The tip will pass easily through the epidermis: first the stratum corneum – the layer of dead cells on the surface and then through the living cells of the stratum germinativan on to the basal layer. Next comes the dermis and pain will now be felt. For here are the nerves and blood vessels. On to the yellow adipose – the golden layer, the fat store through which the point will glide with ease. Now it will face sterner opposition as the tendon-tough fascia stand in its way. But once through, the intercostal muscle will be easily penetrated as will the grey layers of the pleura.

Now the missile can set about its business in earnest. Where to go next? The matter may be already decided as the breeching of the vacuum in between the layers of the pleura may cause the collapse of the lungs. There is a paradox though, as the javelin may itself plug the wound, delaying catastrophe until the moment of retrieval. Should the lungs be spared and the javelin take a central route into the mediastinum, then the heart and large vessels stand in the way. The outer epicardium layer will do its best to arrest progress, but breeched, the heart-beating myocardium layer is next and finally the endocardium. Now there is nothing to prevent entry into the inner chambers and massive blood loss is certain. It is a matter of time before the pressure drops and the brain is deprived of its life source.

Either way, the tip can continue its journey, encountering each layer in reverse order. If it doesn't avoid the spinal column, it may well smash through it.

Well made, strongly thrown, the javelin will now emerge, once more parting fabric. Assuming it retains enough kinetic energy, it can embed itself in yet more dead tissue – the wood of a barn door for example. And buried deeply enough, it could well hold upright an adolescent male of average weight.

FLORENCE AND THE MACHINE

The two women pushed open the door of Costa and, chatting non-stop, made their way to a table set back from the others in a recess to one side of the entrance. Youngish – certainly this side of forty – they were both dressed in a style that might be called shabby chic. Once seated they leant conspiratorially towards each other, their close proximity suggesting that they knew each other very well indeed.

They met like this on a regular basis, and usually before a council or Labour Party meeting. They had a friendship that dated back to university and one that had been cemented by their mutual interest in left-of-centre – very left of centre – politics. This had taken them from the ideological rigidities of the Socialist Workers Party, through to a brief flirtation with the serious-minded Communist Party and on to membership of the Labour Party, where they were able to enjoy the factional power struggles combined with a raucous social life.

Both had been serious enough to stand for office: Florence now as councillor and Sylvia as secretary of the ward in which they lived. Many of their conversations were about the cut and thrust of politics, but such was the friendship between the two that the talk, accompanied often by much laughter, would drift into more personal matters. Today was such a day.

It was a man of course and there was a problem of course. Florence began confiding in her friend about an affair she had been having with a fellow councillor for several months. Hitherto she had kept the matter secret, thinking that even Sylvia might disapprove of her betrayal of husband Jack, as well as one or two other things. Recently though, Sylvia had probed her friend with great persistence, having noticed her upbeat mood and the sparkle in her eyes.

In fact Florence, having decided that this would be the moment to come clean, could hardly wait to get matters off her chest.

"It sounds silly, but he makes me laugh. They did that research once, do you remember? It came top of the list of things that attracted a woman to a man – the ability to make us laugh. It seems that they've programmed that into him and very successfully too. You should hear the things he comes up with. I'm not talking about jokes here – not that he can't tell some very funny ones. No, he is somehow able to take something I've said, even a worry, and in a delicate and charming way show me the funny side without at all diminishing it. I love that."

"Yeah, all well and good but what about, you know, the other side of things?" said Sylvia. She winked provocatively, teasing her friend.

What she hadn't expected was that Florence would be quite so forthcoming. But Florence, glancing around to make sure that no one else was in earshot, wanted to talk:

"I'm not telling tales out of school, but Jack was not exactly insatiable, if you know what I mean. Once a week was more than enough for him and even then he went straight off to sleep afterwards." She blushed before admitting: "I find as I've got older, that I've become, you know, more interested in that sort of thing."

Sylvia, slightly embarrassed, placed a hand over her friend's. "It's all right Flo, I was teasing. I mean you don't have to ... "

"No I want to. There's more to it than you think." Florence paused briefly, staring down at the table before continuing in a whispered torrent. She was trying to be light, jokey even, but Sylvia realised that this was just a preamble, something to be hurried through before ... what? She was far from certain that she wanted to know, her unease compounded by a looming sense of guilt. Shaking her head, she switched her attention back to what Florence was telling her:

" ... 27 is tireless of course. He has been programmed to give a woman every attention and, not only that, to learn down to the finest detail what it is that floats my boat. I know it sounds kind of weird but, really, they've thought of everything where these guys are concerned. His software is anything but, if you get my drift. Any time there has been a hint of a problem – a slowing down at a crucial moment for example – I just switch him off, switch him on again and we're ready to rock and roll. I'm exhausted but in a good way!"

Sylvia tried to emulate her friend's tone, aware that it was just a delaying tactic.

"I bet you are you dirty cow," she said.

They both laughed uncertainly, but quickly fell silent. Florence stared again at the table with a frown of concentration deepening on her face and then continued, her tone more serious.

"No listen, this is important. I've never felt this way before about anyone, certainly not Jack. All Jack really cares about in the end is himself. 27 seems to care about *me*."

"Whoa there girl," interrupted Sylvia, "let's not get carried away. This is a machine we're talking about – you know, just a machine."

"I know, I know," said Florence burying her head in her hands. "The sex is great and all that and I'd think of 27 as an oversize vibrator if it wasn't for … all the rest. It's so nice to have someone take so much interest. He really does seem to care. And here's another thing, he doesn't seem to want anything in return. I mean, Jack is like a kid in that respect – totally self-centred and needy. 27 gives, gives and gives again. He is totally focussed on me and, I'll be honest, it feels great. I mean, for the first time in my life I feel lov…."

"Oh for Christ' sake Flo. Just listen to yourself. Get real! You know as well as I do how this works. The buggers are programmed for God's sake! I mean usually for all the political stuff – after all they have a job to do and…"

"You don't understand," wailed Florence beginning to get a bit teary now. "It's all so intimate, he seems to know me better than…"

"Of course he does," Sylvia snapped back, shrieking a little in exasperation. "He's programmed to learn, to build up a more and more complex understanding…"

The two sat upright in their seats, their backing away a subconscious indication that they, the best of friends, were coming close to arguing, and neither wanted that. After a minute or so of silence while they sipped ruefully at their coffee, Sylvia spoke again, this time in more thoughtful tones:

"You know what occurs to me Flo? If we agree that these

bots are what we make them, then you have to ask two questions: How come the programmers know so much about you? And, if the knowledge is becoming more sophisticated and intimate, then who is updating the information if it's not you?"

"I know you're right Sylv," replied Florence, "It's stuff I've never talked to anyone about, except you of course. I mean it's as though he can read my mind."

Another silence followed and then Florence, lifting her head, gazed directly into her friend's eyes. The moment for the no-longer-to-be-delayed revelation had come.

"Sylv…" She hesitated, gathering courage. "I haven't told you the worst part. You don't know 27 do you?"

"No. Though to be honest, they all look alike to me, I mean some sit on our side of the chamber and some on the other but apart from that…I have to say that I've sure as hell never fancied one, not like you seem to be doing."

"Look, don't hate me for this…"

"Just say it Flo. I *am* your friend"

"He's…he's…he's one of them. The other side. You know, he's a Tory."

This time Sylvia *was* shocked. She stared in disbelief at her friend who, with cheeks ablaze, had dropped her gaze to the fidgeting hands in her lap.

They had come up together through the party ranks from student activists to hard-working constituency members. Although Florence had finally made it to the city council, Sylvia remained a stalwart in the day-to-day running of the party and in particular was a constant support to her friend in matters both personal and ideological. It was surely just a matter of time before she too took her place in the chamber.

Both women had fiercely opposed the introduction of Cobots but a combination of savage cuts in the public sector in the first two decades of the century, plus massive advances in robot technology in the same period, had made it inevitable. Even they had to admit that there were many functions of local government that were utterly routine and well-suited to cybernetic intervention. Their objections had been specifically about the inflexibility and lack of subtlety in artificial intelligence – the inability to think outside the box as it were.

With a human being there was always the possibility, one way or another, of changing the hardness of, or modifying, a point of view. You could reason, cajole, bully, blackmail, entreat, plead or command. You could offer power, bribes or the share of a bed. Cobots were, on the whole, immune to such pressures. True, there was much fun to be had from skewing your debating points in a way that influenced the learning faculty they had. At the last full council meeting, members of all parties had taunted the last remaining UKIP bot, already over-loaded with inflammatory and contradictory data. This had resulted in a spectacular melt-down, necessitating the clearing of the chamber while the smouldering remains were dealt with. On the whole, though, the whips made damn sure that on essential matters of policy, the programming of their bots was faithful to the party line and that come voting time, loyalty was assured. This was true of both Labour and Tory bots.

A clumsy attempt had been made to maintain democratic integrity. The Cobots were allotted in exact proportion to the vote for humans but this contained a flaw that was much discussed. A vote for four members of one party and two of another results in a majority of two. Simply replicating those figures with robots, which was the carelessly thought-through procedure, multiplied to eight and four and a majority of four. It was a crudity that tended to entrench the party in power and give it voting muscle that it otherwise would not have had.

So it was that the incumbent Tories had, after two years, exacted on the city a brutal regime of cuts in services, social housing and other amenities. They had also turned back to policies much beloved by the Tory faithful, including the reintroduction of selection in the better local schools, and the ending of funding to sexual and racial minority groups as well as to the arts. On the other hand, policing had been pumped full of extra resource along with a plethora of CCTV and other snooping paraphernalia. Such was the record of No 27 and his cronies.

Sylvia sat stock-still and appeared to hold her breath for a full half minute before releasing it with a long drawn out "Fffffffffuck!" Her anger had returned but there was something else as well.

"Are you out of your mind girl? Have you forgotten what these shits have done in this town. I'm sorry, but I don't care if he does ring your bells ... it's just out of order – disgusting in fact."

Florence burst into tears. "Sylv, don't be like that. Pleeeease. I don't know who else to talk to."

"What about Jack? What's Jack going to say when he finds out?" snapped Sylvia.

"I told you, it's over with Jack. He's useless in bed. He doesn't understand me. He doesn't even like me for God's sake. Fuck Jack."

"You can say what you like about Jack but at least he's stuck to his guns politically. It's one thing being cheated on, but with a Tory! He'll be devastated. What were you thinking ? For God's sake, there are plenty of decent guys out there – you know, good-looking, intelligent and, more to the point, politically sound! Oh, and have I missed something? – yes, some of them are living breathing human beings, not some fucking machine."

Their attempt at discretion had been forgotten and heads turned at the sound of Sylvia's raised voice and salty language. The falling out they had struggled to avoid was swift to follow. Florence, her face running with tears, stood abruptly to her feet, knocked over her chair and, grabbing her bag, turned and ran from the café.

Sylvia lowered her head into her hands and sat motionless for several minutes. Then, rising suddenly to her feet, she threw her coat on, pushed through the doors, and strode purposively down the street.

She, thank God, had a great relationship with boyfriend Clive who, as well as being a human, seemed to embody all the virtues, both carnal and new-mannish, that the saintly 27 apparently displayed. Somewhere at the back of her mind, she suspected that much of her anger was that a mere machine could be thought the equal of Clive. But something else was starting to bother her. It bothered her a lot.

Clive was, by profession, a computer programmer but went also under the nom de keyboard 'superslash' and was something of a renowned hacker. They had met, though, as members of the Labour Party. It was his job to translate party policy into programmed instructions for the Labour bots.

She pushed open the door of the flat they shared, just a stone's throw from the town hall.

"Clive, Clive, I need to talk to you. Where are you?" He was where he always was – crouched intently over his computer in his darkened study.

"What is it babe? Christ you look terrible. What's up?"

"Oh Clive," she wailed, "What have we done? More to the point, what have you done?"

"Me, why me? What are you talking about?"

"You remember that thing I asked if you could do a few months ago? You know that bot thing. Remember, my friend Flo had been going on and on about how useless her husband was. Week after week I got that stuff from her. She became increasingly miserable and, frankly, no fun to be with anymore. I just thought she needed a smile on her face – you know, a good fuck and a guy that made her laugh – listened to her for Christ's sake."

"So," said Clive, remembering, "I did what you asked – hacked into a bot. You came up with the inside info. I just cued the bugger up, gave him the necessary face and voice recognition. It was simple. Why, what's wrong?"

"She thinks she's in love with him – that's what's wrong. She was so desperate for attention that she was bowled over by all the bullshit."

"I wouldn't call it bullshit," protested Clive. "I mean I made him like me – you know none of that hairy ape-man bollocks. A caring, sharing sort of guy."

"Go on, why don't you blow your own trumpet while you're at it? Well here's the thing clever dick – you fouled up. You hacked into a Tory!"

"That's right, you asked me to – C27. I thought it was odd. I just assumed it was part of the kick, you know, like a perversion. Sleeping with the enemy if you like."

"Idiot. You know full well what the C stands for – Conservative, though I can think of another C word that fits the bill!" Anyway I told you L27. L27. L for Labour – got it?"

"You didn't babe, you definitely said…"

"I'm not arguing with you Clive but we've got to sort this mess out. Come on, you've got work to do."

Several days had passed since the friends had met over coffee. Florence was due to speak as Labour spokesperson for personnel matters at an extraordinary meeting of the Policy and Resources Committee. On the table was a change of standing orders concerning recognition of trade union branches and the encouragement of an alternative staff association. This was a classic Tory policy aimed at the continued undermining of the unions. But Florence was in her element and her task was to speak for and propose an amendment to maintain existing agreements. There had been no question of meeting up with C27 and she had, instead, used all her available time working on her speech.

The arguments had been raging back and forth for a full hour. To Sylvia, who was observing, the Labour amendment seemed to be making ground despite the Tory majority. As far as she could tell, the more moderate human councillors were beginning to waver – not the robot Tories of course, they would be responding according to the programming controlled by the whips.

She had come for two reasons. Firstly, she was supporting Florence and secondly, this was her first opportunity to check that Clive had done what he said he would.

For the first half of her speech, Florence had been in good impassioned form but when she got to her key points – maintaining good industrial relations, the retention of real democracy in the workplace, nurturing human resources – the heckling began:

"Calm down dear – just stick to the facts," was the first intervention. All heads turned to see who was speaking. C27 had risen to his feet and was waving his papers. Florence paused for just a moment and then ploughed on.

"Councillor Jenkins should check her diary. This might be the wrong time of the month to engage in rational discussion." A hush fell on the chamber. This was a bit much for even the most Neanderthal of politicians.

Florence responded with a quiet put-down.

"You should know 27, or should I call you 7?" This got an appreciative chuckle from both sides of the chamber, though they were unlikely to have fully understood the implication.

There was more from 27.

"Surely Councillor Jenkins has better things to do with her time – doesn't she have a family waiting at home? Put your boss on, maybe he can do better."

Florence, realising that silence greeted each interjection, shrewdly stopped responding and let the chair issue warnings to C27. These he ignored and eventually Labour protests successfully had him ejected from the chamber.

Sylvia had waited for her friend on the front steps of the town hall. Florence emerged surrounded by a group of fellow councillors all bubbling with noisy excitement. The Labour amendment, against the odds, had been accepted. This was due in no small part to Florence's well-argued presentation, her calm in the face of outrageous interruptions, and the unexpected shift in opinion by a significant number on the opposite bench. A sympathy vote maybe, but Florence, eyes gleaming with triumph, was acknowledging the victory however it had come about.

Sylvia virtually lifted Florence off her feet with her congratulatory hug.

"Well done Flo. What a triumph. You were brilliant, just brilliant. Do you fancy a celebratory pint or … ", and here she adopted a deeply ironic tone, " … are you off to see C27?"

"You what?" replied Florence, "Fuck him." "I'll tell you what though Sylv, did you see the way L27 was eying me up. I think I've made a real impression there. I'll have that pint first though!"

SEADOG

The face is Rushmore still; the skin like hammered copper. The imperiously hooked nose is just a hair's breadth below the lid that is lifted and dropped above it. Lifted and dropped. Bang bang bang. With each lift the light flickers in, glinting off the waxen ridges of forehead, nose, cheeks and lips. As if there were any doubt, the eyes attest to the absence of life. They stare wide, the colour and texture of soft cheese skin.

A child's fingers grasp the edge of the lid of the sea chest, lifting and dropping, lifting and dropping. Bang bang bang. They belong to Tom. He is eleven years old, though his sturdy build and ruddy features make him seem older. The same is true of his twin, Melanie who stands by the door of the bedroom. She is laughing and, by knocking on the door panel, seems to be mimicking the noise he is making. She stops for a moment and wrinkles her nose in mock disgust.

"Ooh, you've farted?" she says. And indeed a sickly smell has pervaded the room.

"No, you have," says Tom and at that the two dissolve into laughter.

Downstairs, the grownups talk in the living room in voices tight with anxiety, The twins' mother, Pamela is there of course along with her sister Beryl who lives in the house next door. They too are twins. They sit opposite each other, leaning forward until their heads almost touch so that they can speak without being overheard. They are forty years old, though fifty to look at. Pam twists a handkerchief in her restless hands as she speaks. Beryl by contrast sits as if frozen. Her husband David is there too. A pudgy and placid fellow, he sits to one side, staring out of the window detached, by request or maybe choice, from the conversation.

"…so what I'm saying is this…for God's sake, what is that row? David, can't you tell them to be quiet? We need to concentrate. This is serious."

David leaves the room to go and check on the kids and returns quickly.

"They're amusing themselves. I mean sure they know how annoying they're being but they're having a laugh. You know how kids are."

"But what are they doing?"

"Well – banging on things – you know – the door, the sea chest."

"Oh Christ," says Pam blenching "Oh sweet Christ." She gets to her feet and, pushing past David, hurries up the stairs to the bedroom.

"You two – how many times must I tell you? This is your grandfathers's room and it's private. If you want to play, go outside or into your own room and for God's sake do something quiet. We're having an important grown-up talk downstairs. Very important."

The children back out of the room as far as the doorway, watching their mother intently. She pauses for a moment and checks the room, relieved to see that nothing has been obviously disturbed. There are the bottled ships, the brass name-plates from vessels long gone. There are the framed sea charts, the brass telescope and the sextant that she doubted the old man really knew how to use. Satisfied, she runs her hands firmly over the lid of the old sea chest as if to emphasise its inviolate status, her eyes brimming with tears. Wrinkling her nose at the fetid air, she looks accusingly at her children and her anger rushes back in. Pushing them out of the room, she slams the door shut and grabbing them by an arm each, she marches them back to their own room at the end of the corridor.

"Ow you're hurting me," yowls Melanie.

"Don't you ever let me catch you in there again. Do you understand?" says her mother, angrily.

After their mother has stamped back down to the living room, a minute passes in silence. Then the door to their room opens tentatively and the two children creep quietly to the top of the stairs where, settling against the railings, they bow their heads in concentration and listen as best they can to the voices below.

" … what are we going to do about him? I knew it would end like this."

"Well, we can't leave things as they are. The police will nose round sooner or later. What are we going to tell them?"

"The stupid, stupid old man – I should think he's laughing at us right now."

"Hardly Beryl – hardly."

"You know what I mean. The old goat always thought we were a couple of useless girlies – not the tough-nut sons he really wanted. This would confirm it – the panic, the indecision. Oh he's laughing all right. What the hell're we going to do Pam?"

"We've got to get rid of him, that's for sure. There must be a place somewhere that would take him. Come on think!"

Such is the children's concentration that they forget that they are supposed to be quiet and begin their knocking again on the railings. Tap tap tap from Tom. Tap tap tap from Mel.

Their mother's voice rises from below, angrier than ever.

"How many times do I have to tell you two? Shut that bloody row!" And then to the others, "Why do they have to do that?" At that she closes the sitting room door firmly, voices are lowered and, for the moment, the children can hear no more of the conversation.

And what of the man of whom they speak? He lies comfortable on a bed of blankets, staring sightlessly at the underside of the sea chest lid. Jerrod is his name, or rather was. The hawk-like set of his features and metal-hammered skin is only partly due to death but also speaks of a life led at sea; to sun and salt spray.

He was the father of Pam and Beryl and grandfather to Tom and Melanie. He never quite left the sea. When he finished on the trawlers, he spent every waking hour down at the harbour, lovingly maintaining his old 'put put' boat and mending his lobster pots. There he would talk to anyone who would give him the time of day, recounting stories, some true, of his sea-faring days.

There were no more avid listeners than Tom and Melanie who, quite young, would be left in his care after school while their parents were still at work. And it wasn't just the stories of his time as fisherman, harpoonist and ship's radio operator that enthralled them. Most days, unless conditions were really bad, he would strap them into their life jackets (he refused to wear one himself) and take them on a trip round the harbour, even allowing them to steer the boat for a while.

They were devoted to this interesting old man. Whereas the learning they did at school seemed to them to be of little practical use, granddad's teachings were quite the opposite: how to set the mackerel hooks and cook the fish over a beach fire; where to lay the lobster pots; how to tie amazing knots; how to forecast the weather just by looking at the clouds and sniffing the wind; how to semaphore or send Morse code; how to mend a net. So many things.

In those days he lived in a tiny fisherman's cottage close to the beach. They adored going there. The front was built from pebbles and then painted black so that it looked like bubbling tar. Inside, the dark rooms were fitted out, to their minds, like a ship's cabin, the furniture looking like it had been assembled from driftwood. Among the nets and stuffed seabirds that lay about the place were models of ships of all kinds. All of them had been made by the old man and he encouraged them to do likewise, even showing them how to get a full-masted schooner into a narrow-necked bottle. They thought this nothing short of miraculous.

He played a rudimentary squeeze box too and he knew many old songs and shanties. Among those he taught them, and which they sang happily for hours on end, were a few 'bawdy' numbers which he made them promise not to perform in front of their parents, although, still young, they barely understood why.

As they approached their tenth birthday and he his eightieth, the old man suffered a minor stroke and it was thought time for him to leave his beloved cottage and come and live with them. He would have a room in their house but with aunty Beryl and uncle David living next door, the care could be shared.

The children were initially delighted to have their grandfather as a fulltime companion but he had been moved against his will and proved a cantankerous and argumentative housemate. True, his antagonism was not directed at the children but his battles with his daughters created an unpleasant atmosphere for all of them. Pam and Beryl were taken aback by just how irritating they found their father, especially since they had suggested the move with the best of intentions. He refused to take the medicine that had been prescribed after his illness, he refused to curb his love of rum after being told to moderate his intake by the doctor, he refused to use a stick now that his knees had started to weaken, claiming that it would make him look old. He wasn't hearing so well and refused to wear a hearing aid for the same reason. He was forever losing his glasses and claiming that he could see perfectly well without them. Then he would forget what he had been told from one moment to the next. His daughters tried to understand, they really did. This was to be expected of elderly people – a loss of short-term memory, but when, again, he denied he had a problem and claimed to have the memory of a twenty-year-old, one or other or both of them would snap and another huge argument would ensue. When that happened he had a way of exacting revenge.

He would disappear without a word. This might be just for a

few hours but sometimes after a particularly virulent argument it could be for a day or two. On such occasions they had no alternative but to phone the police, who had grown wearily used to such calls. They had found the old man, variously, bunking with one of his old sea-faring pals, dead drunk in the local A&E or fast asleep beneath the tarpaulin of his beached boat.

At first the kids stood by him, defending him when the adults became exasperated, but as their eleventh year approached, things gradually changed for them too. Their grandfather had always treated them as one and made no distinction between brother and sister. Both had listened to his stories, sang his songs and shared the same tasks and chores either at sea or back in the cottage. And of course they felt themselves to be one – inseparable since birth and self-sufficient from an early age. It ran in the family – their mother and auntie Beryl had been just such twins brought up largely by their querulous father after his timid brow-beaten wife had died, exhausted, just shy of thirty-seven.

Now, and very gradually, he sought to separate his grandchildren, one from the other. Tom he would take out in the boat on his own, no longer within the sheltered confines of the harbour but out to rougher seas. When Tom asked why Mel wasn't coming, he would reply, "T'aint women's work Tom – she'm better orf at 'ome ."

It wasn't as though he was unkind to Mel. On the contrary, he made a great fuss of her and began to buy her little things, "So's you don't mind not comin' wi us". He would give her sweets, magazines and, on one occasion, a tiny kitten. She shared these treasures with Tom of course, but was puzzled and hurt by the change.

For their part, they felt obliged to go along with the old man's whims. He was not to be argued with. But if he thought, or indeed intended, that a wedge should be driven between them, then he was mistaken. If anything, the time apart made keener their desire to be together, to support each other absolutely. It is not uncommon in twins but others remarked on the intensity in their case. Some found it unsettling.

And then something happened to Mel. Something that upset her a great deal. Something she confided to her mother, who responded with sudden angry tears and called her daughter 'a wicked liar'. Melanie didn't persist with her mother but did, as always, confide in Tom.

Now the old man was gone.

Mel and Tom have gravitated to the foot of the stairs, opposite the living room door, which has come slightly ajar. They sit looking unconcernedly at the walls as though bored but both are listening intently to the conversation, which, though hoarsely whispered, can be heard once more. Through the gap they can see their mother and aunt with their heads close together.

First they hear their mother.

"We have to report him missing. They won't do anything, they're fed up with us for sure but it does put us in the clear – it shows we've tried our best."

Then auntie Beryl – her voice high-pitched and full of sudden anger.

"God I hated him – he deserves the worst. I'll say it if you won't – I'd be happy never to set eyes on him again."

"Look B I agree, of course I do, but we have to get our stories straight. We argued, he stamped out of the house in a fury and we haven't seen or heard from him for a week."

"That's all very well but it leaves us with (Beryl mouths the words) *a big problem.* It won't look right if we aren't seen to look in the usual places – you know drop in on a few of his mates, check the boat."

"Yes you're right, we have to make it look like we tried."

There is a pause in the conversation and then their mother's bravado seems to collapse. She drops her head into her hands and tries unsuccessfully to suppress a violent sobbing. The children watch as aunt Beryl rises to her feet and holds her sister tightly.

"I know love, I know. He was a hateful man. Those things he did to you. I believed you, even if ma didn't. He was disgusting. It wasn't your fault love – it was never your fault. It's all over now. Hush, hush."

"Why me?" wails their mother

"I don't know love. Maybe you were more naïve. He tried it with me too but just the once. Put his hand (she mouths the words again) *up my dress.* I yelled blue murder at him. I was so bloody angry. I think I frightened him."

There is another silence and then their mother's voice bursts out, now with a note of triumph

"I can't believe he's gone for good."

The sisters cling together and began a caterwauling in which it's difficult to separate sobs from laughter.

At the foot of the stairs, the twins are also looking at each other but with quiet smiles of triumph on their faces. And their tapping has started up again – a mixture of soft thumps made with the flat-out fingers of one hand and sharper sounds made with finger nails of the other. The old man had taught them well.

Tom: Dah Di-di-di-dit Dit Dah-di-dah-dah, Dah-di-dit Dah-dah-dah, Dah-dit Dah-dah-dah Dah, Dah-di-dah Dah-dit Dah-dah-dah Di-dah-dah, Di-di-di-dit Dit, Di-dit Di-di-dit, Dah-di-dit Dit Di-dah Dah-di-dit
[THEY DO NOT KNOW HE IS DEAD]

Mel: Di-dah-dah Di-di-di-dit Di-dah Dah, Di-di-dit Di-di-dit Di-dah Di-dah-di-dit Di-dah-di-dit, Di-dah-dah Dit, Dah-di-dit Dah-dah-dah, Dah-dit Dah-dah-dah Di-dah-dah Di-di-dah-dah-di-dit
[WHAT SHALL WE DO NOW?]

Tom: Di-dah-dah Di-dah Di-dit Dah, Di-di-dah Dah-dit Dah Di-dit Di-dah-di-dit, Dah Di-di-di-dit Dit Dah-di-dah-dah, Dah-dah-dit Dah-dah-dah, Dah-dah-dah Di-di-dah Dah
[WAIT UNTIL THEY GO OUT]

Mel: Di-dah-dah Di-di-di-dit Di-dah Dah, Dah Di-di-di-dit Dit Dah-dit Di-di-dah-dah-di-dit
[WHAT THEN?]

Tom: Di-dah-dah-dit Di-di-dah Dah, Di-di-di-dit Di-dit Dah-dah, Di-dit Dah-dit, Dah Di-di-di-dit Dit, Di-dah-dah Di-di-di-dit Dit Dit Di-dah-di-dit Dah-di-di-dit Di-dah Di-dah-dit Di-dah-dit Dah-dah-dah Di-dah-dah
[PUT HIM IN THE WHEELBARROW]

Mel: Di-dah-dah Di-di-di-dit Di-dah Dah, Dah Di-di-di-dit
Dit Dah-dit Di-di-dah-dah-di-dit
[WHAT THEN?]

Tom: Dah Di-dit Di-dah-dah-dit, Di-di-di-dit Di-dit Dah-dah,
Di-dit Dah-dit, Dah Di-di-di-dit Dit, Di-di-dit Dit Di-dah
[TIP HIM IN THE SEA]

Mel: Dah Di-di-di-dit Dit, Di-dah-dah-dit Dah-dah-dah Di-
dit Di-di-dit Dah-dah-dah Dah-dit, Di-dah-dit Di-di-dah
Dah-dah Di-di-dah-dah-di-dit
[THE POISON RUM?]

Tom: Di-dit, Di-dah-dah-dit Dah-dah-dah Di-di-dah Di-
dah-dit Dit Dah-di-dit, Di-dit Dah, Dah-di-dit Dah-dah-dah
Di-dah-dah Dah-dit, Dah Di-di-di-dit Dit, Di-di-dit Di-dit
Dah-dit Dah-di-dah
[I POURED IT DOWN THE SINK]

Mel: Dah Di-di-di-dit Di-dah Dah-dit Dah-di-dah, Dah-di-
dah-dah Dah-dah-dah Di-di-dah
[THANK YOU]

Tom: Di-di-di-dit Dit, Dah-di-dit Dit Di-di-dit Dit Di-dah-
dit Di-di-di-dah Dit Dah-di-dit, Di-dit Dah
[HE DESERVED IT]
Mel: Di-di-di-dit Dit, Dah Dah-dah-dah Di-di-dah Dah-di-
dah-dit Di-di-di-dit Dit Dah-di-dit, Dah-dah Dit
[HE TOUCHED ME]

60

Tom: Dah-di-dit Di-dit Di-dah-dit Dah Dah-di-dah-dah,
Dah-di-dit Dah-dah-dah Dah-dah-dit
[DIRTY DOG]

HIGH FLYER

Mid afternoon and the sun was not yet hot enough to make his run uncomfortable. On the contrary there was the lightest of breezes, alternately warming and cooling him as he negotiated the cliff-top path. The sea, four hundred feet below, glittered with a thousand points of light, each demanding his attention. His deep rhythmic breathing took in the scent of grass fattened by recent rains and, more powerfully, the heady notes of wild thyme bruised under foot as he pounded over the undulating downland.

Nick thought, not for the first time, how extraordinarily blessed he was. He had turned fifty just a few weeks before and could be forgiven for taking it easy now, enjoying the rewards that hard work and a successful career had brought him. Yet here he was on his favourite run – the cliff-top path running between Dover and St Margaret's Bay. Until recently, friends of his would have joined him but, one by one, they had given up, complaining about painful knees, debilitating weight or simply lack of time. He, on the other hand, had never felt better.

He had tried to explain to non-runners the 'spiritual' aspect of his running but embarrassed himself as soon as he started to use that kind of language. And yet, and yet, how else could this feeling of wellbeing be explained? Some suggested endorphins, the body's natural opiates. Well maybe, but that was only part of it.

On a day like this, feeling great for his age and skittering at a brisk pace up and down the soft green path, gazing out beyond the glitter-ball sea to the distant blue horizon, it felt perfect. It doesn't get any better than this, he thought.

The cliff-top path is popular with runners and walkers alike. From the east of the town's promenade there are the remains of the old town at the foot of the mighty cliffs on which the castle stands. Beyond, a series of steps rise steeply up the cliff side, passing first beneath the stanchions of the trunk road carrying freight lorries to and from the Eastern Dock that can be seen in endless turmoil far below. From there a well-defined path passes a visitor's centre before rougher trails snake out over the grassy downland that tops the cliffs.

Although the route rises and drops steeply, the overall tendency is upwards, the highest point being nearly 400 feet above the sea at Fan Bay. Soon, the South Foreland Lighthouse comes into view – a popular turning point for the less ambitious. Beyond that the path plummets down for a mile or so to the bleak foreshore at St Margaret's Bay. Turn here, back for Dover, and the keen runner can be satisfied with a challenging nine-mile workout.

The cliff edge scallops in and out along its length with a less-trodden narrow path following its line. Walkers are warned to avoid the crumbling cliff edge and most avoid this option. The main path keeps well back from the edge, scribing a median route between high points. This latter was the one he normally took, preferring not to have to watch his step but to 'switch off' and experience the uncomplicated pleasure of running.

It doesn't get any better, he had thought, and yet, as he ran the safe path, he began to look, in a way he hadn't before, at the path that followed the edge. The lush grass was barely flattened by the feet of the brave few who had gone that way but it followed an enticingly sinuous line rising up and down, in and out with the shape of the cliff. On such a day, how could he resist? He cut across to the edge. The ground was instantly softer and the grass squeaked under his feet as though reciprocating his touch, releasing even stronger scents. As he ran, scatterings of chalkhill blues danced in front of him, and the way was marked with tufts of golden grass which, catching the light, glowed more like silver. Among them, yellow vetch bought brilliant colour to the slopes with, here and there, a shock of purple orchid showing.

His legs were feeling fantastic – so strong. On the rising sections where normally he would have to work hard and deal with lactic acid building in his muscles, he seemed able to bound up the slopes with ease and, facing toward the sun, he had the impression of ascending into the light. As he ran to its centre, it seemed to reach above and around him in a brilliant embrace. It doesn't get any better, he repeated to himself.

The downhill sections were especially thrilling. The path swooped to the very edge, giving a delicious sensation of danger as the pace inevitably picked up. He had to consciously slow before turning away and up again on the next rise. It was like riding waves. It couldn't get any better. He found himself whooping ecstatically like a child, not something he normally did, and then tears of happiness welled up, taking him further by surprise.

The gulls zig-zagging on the warm currents swirling up and around the cliff face seemed to be experiencing the same joy that he was. If there was a purpose to their criss-cross antics, he did not know it, save for the sheer pleasure in movement that he himself was feeling.

It was the kestrel he encountered, though, that most accurately reflected his state of mind. It seemed to view the excitable gulls with distain, hanging absolutely still in the air, wings outstretched, the uplift perfectly judged against its own weight. It seemed to have time in its thrall – to have stopped it at the perfect point; the moment held in utter equilibrium, not to be bettered.

As he ran, he started thinking more about his life. In every way he thought of himself as being gifted with extraordinary good fortune. It wasn't just his pleasure in good health and the privilege of being able to run the landscape in this way but every other aspect. He was not a religious man but sometimes wished there was someone he could thank for being the beneficiary of such munificence.

He had met his wife Lucy at university just as they were completing their final term. Friends joked about them being the 'golden couple', not with bitterness or envy but in simple acknowledgement that, of their circle, they were the most attractive and the most likely to succeed, not just in their chosen careers but in love and life as a whole. Both sets of parents remained alive and in good health and their own children were embarked on promising careers.

It may have been the trip over a clump of grass, which slightly turned his ankle, or the momentary hiding of the sun behind a cloud, but in an instant his mood changed. The tears in his eyes had remained but in that instant the emotion that had fermented them mutated from joy to self-pity.

Suddenly the uphill climbs took on a Sisyphean aspect – one of pointless effort. The downhills became a metaphoric reflection of his plunging spirits. He ran on, shaking his head, not quite understanding what had just happened to him and desperately trying to recover his former good spirits.

The understanding, when it came, hit him like a punch. Not only could life not get any better – it was difficult to imagine how – but having reached the high point in his run, as in his life, he could not avoid a downward trajectory. Logic demanded no less.

The smug litany of his self satisfactions from just minutes before now gave way to thoughts of an altogether darker hue. Would Lucy tire of him, of the perfection of their lives even, and embark on an affair? Would one or other of their parents become infirm and in need of care? Would he find a redundancy letter waiting for him? And, oh, merciful god – would one of his kids have some terrible accident?

The thoughts that assailed him now would not leave, and depression encompassed him just as the cloud had obscured the sun. How could he preserve the perfection of his life? He couldn't bear the thought that things must, by degree, become worse.

The swooping downhill runs now took on a different character. With each, a pain rose in his chest as he slithered towards the edge, tears obscuring his view and sobs constricting his breathing. He knew he should return to the safe path but the synchronicity between the plunging path and his plummeting spirits held him in curious fascination. He tried hard to bring to mind the recent feelings of harmony and joy: the beautiful light, the effortless surfing of the ups and downs, the kestrel hovering still and perfect in the air above the sea, and asked himself again and again: "How can I keep things as they are?".

He stopped, hands on knees, breathing hard and then, turning, looked back up the path. The highest point was still catching the sunlight and, caught in its glow was the kestrel. It remained pinned to the sky, wings outstretched, unmoving, holding time still.

It seemed he had no choice. He ran back up: back to the peak, back to the light, back to the kestrel hovering beyond the cliff's edge.

THE GODLESS HOUR

His drinking had taken hold again. It didn't take much. Any excuse would do. There had been attempts to modify it. He could and did go for days without a drop but, as always, he got to a point where he began to congratulate himself on the strength of his will; to persuade himself that he was no alcoholic; that unlike those that were, he could stop whenever he chose to and without difficulty. That being so, it didn't matter if he (lapsed wasn't the right word) – *chose* to have a glass of something. There were, after all, many legitimate reasons why one might want to do so: drink as balm, drink as medicine, drink as celebration. The reasons and excuses had queued up and jostled for attention. Almost six months had passed since he last abstained and then just for a night or two.

There was the pressure at work. He had tied himself to a loser's contract with a stationery supply firm. On a miserable basic salary, he was required to spend his days working the telephone in an attempt to drum up new business, the balance of his income being made up with commission on sales. The recession had undermined the potential market considerably and as he himself sounded more and more desperate with his pitch, so the voices at the other end of the line grew more abusive and angry at his, among many such calls.

As his commissions diminished month by month and his

bills became more difficult to honour, he found it increasingly necessary to relieve the stress with a glass or three of something at the end of the working day. Plenty of people did that. It was a sensible use of alcohol wasn't it? How else was one to draw a line between the grind of the day and a hoped-for evening of relaxation? Okay, maybe the quick slug of vodka in the morning before making his first call was taking things too far, but he had hoped it would make him sound more relaxed and therefore trustworthy to potential clients.

It hadn't worked. He was on his second warning. His boss, an otherwise forgiving soul, and one not averse himself to a pint or two after work, had taken him aside on the first occasion and made it clear that his poor success record was not entirely due to the economic downturn. Then, he had been sympathetic and had given the official warning reluctantly. On the second occasion some months later, his advice having been ignored, he gave the warning without as much as making eye contact.

Jenny's departure had been preceded by a similar pattern. Initially she had been solicitous, thinking that with love alone she could coax him into a behavioural change. Then, when one too many promises had been made and broken, she started to nag, something that infuriated him and, if anything, gave him further reason to fill his glass.

Sex had been an early casualty. Jenny, ten years younger than him had been an enthusiastic and inventive partner at the start of their relationship, but drink, as he remembered from his school Shakespeare, "…provokes the desire, but it takes away the performance", and after one too many nights of frustration and humiliation he had awoken to find her wardrobe cleared and she gone. She hadn't even left a note. There was no need.

It hadn't taken long for their tiny rented flat to deteriorate. Jenny had been a conscientious housekeeper. This had not simply been the result of long-established habit. Keeping the place clean and tidy was something that she could control, just as Ken's unravelling was something she could not. He was not immune to the chaos around him, indeed he had, in earlier days, been just as house-proud. Now he saw what needed doing and resolved to tackle the accumulating tasks systematically – tomorrow, or just as soon as he could find the time.

He woke from a disturbed sleep on the living room sofa, throat dry and eyes aching. He was fully dressed and his clothes stank of sweat, smoke and alcohol, testament to a long evening spent at a pub near his office whence he had no memory of returning home. As he stood unsteadily, food cartons and cans crunched and clattered under foot and he kicked them angrily aside, regretting the sudden movement as pain shot through his head.

He looked at the mantelpiece clock. Three a.m. Of all times, this was the most god-awful. The alcohol had worn off leaving him racked; there had not been enough sleep to get him through the worst and there were many night hours left before he would feel justified in reaching for the hair of the dog. As he stood there swaying, something came to mind. It was a few half-remembered lines that he had been made to learn at school or maybe from a play he had appeared in. He had been quite keen on that sort of thing back then. How did it go?

"…something, something, something…in the hours that some call godless, the tribulations that beset a man weigh heavy as stone. 'tis a weight to be borne or be borne down by alone…"

He couldn't remember who had written it. Was it Shakespeare again or the Bible maybe? He wished he hadn't remembered at all, especially as it went on:

"…most await the healing sun, whose rays that same stone warms…something, something…but pity those, who weak with woe, by potion, rope or fall, another path do go…"

Oh god, oh god, oh god, he moaned, and before he could stop himself he dropped his head into his hands and was overtaken by yelping sobs that he tried and failed to suppress. After a few minutes and quieter now, he sank back to the sofa and remained sitting there for the rest of the night staring sightlessly at the blank wall.

He needed the 'healing sun' but the morning, when it came, was a killer: leaden skies, strong winds and stinging rain. *His* stone weighed heavy and the gulps of morning vodka did nothing to alleviate a deepening despair. He was gripped by a desperate desire to get out, get away from the squalid surroundings which served only to remind him of himself. Throwing his drink-stained raincoat over crumpled clothes he stumbled through the door he had drunkenly failed to close the night before and out into the cold wet morning.

It was a work day but he knew now that the time had come when he could no more wash, shave and find a clean shirt than his boss would tolerate any further his bumbling, incoherent phone calls. As the rising wind whipped at his clothes, he made instead for the ugliest place he could think of. Why he didn't know. It was as though he was so far down that he needed the misery to be rounded off – made complete.

The Begwell Centre struggled, even in fair weather, to look anything other than a mountain of stained concrete. On a grey day, any form that might just be articulated by light and shade disappeared into lumpen shapelessness. It was an early 60s attempt at a shopping mall, with the entrance level still exhibiting some sign of life – a few chain shops remaining open.

It was the basement level he made for though – the light fading as he clumped down a stalled escalator. It was no longer thought worth heating or lighting this level. The only illumination came from a handful of charity shops that were taking advantage of the minimal rents on offer. Nine out of ten premises were long-closed with heavily graffitied shutters – some buckled and jemmied. The prevailing smell was of urine. In several doorways he passed the sleeping homeless – no more than bundles of rags – and wondered as he did so, how many weeks or days it would be until he joined them.

He scuffled down a particularly abandoned stretch, drawn on into the darkest and coldest place. He noticed a movement ahead of him and slowed as a figure emerged from the shadow.

She was not exceptional in appearance: fortyish, a little overweight, no make-up, untidy hair, dressed Marks and Sparks safe. What he failed to understand was what she was doing in this god-forsaken, shop-forsaken corner of the mall. The thought crumbled as, to his alarm, she made straight for him.

He started to speak, thinking that she had misrecognised him. "I don't…"

"I need you," she said simply.

"Um … I think … "

"I need you," she repeated firmly "Come with me."

She turned and he, hesitating just briefly, began to follow. There was at that moment nowhere else he wanted, or knew where, to go.

He noticed for the first time, between two abandoned shops, a faint light spilling from an opening. The woman turned into it and beckoned for him to follow. A passageway plunged steeply downwards on a sloping ramp. He put his hand out to steady himself and felt only cold rough concrete.

"Where are we going?" he asked.

"I need you," she repeated and scurried on. The passage kept going downwards but at each turn the light grew brighter and the temperature rose.

For several minutes they descended until, turning a final corner, he was forced by a blinding light to shade his eyes. Her hand reached for his and, lifting it gently from his face, led him forward into what appeared to be a large courtyard.

He struggled to understand what he was seeing. The courtyard was bathed in sunlight – real sunlight as far as he could see. He looked up to determine its source. Was it a light well of some kind? Given the weather conditions outside, that didn't quite explain things. It was warming too so didn't feel like mere lighting.

The plants around the cloister-like setting were profuse and succulent, a mixture of shapely palms, and exuberant native species. He recognised giant hostas and salvias, with clematis and roses spiralling up the honeyed stone columns that supported a vine-covered walkway. In the centre was an ornate fountain of the same stone, gently spilling water into a pool plated with flowering lilies. Around the courtyard were many open-faced rooms like summer pergolas. The sun spilled equally into all of them despite them being on opposing sides.

He noticed for the first time that each contained a couple of people seated on cushioned stone benches and that others were strolling across the central courtyard. There were men and women in pairs, men with men and women with women – it seemed quite random but in each case one held the hand of the other and whispered gently, just as his hand was being held and he was being whispered to.

"I need you, I need you."

His body shuddered with a pleasure like stepping into a warm bath on a cold day or feeling the sun emerge finally from behind clouds on a childhood holiday. For whole minutes he stood enjoying the sensation, not wanting to break the spell, and all the while his hand was gently held and the whispers enveloped him like a warm breeze. And then he leant forward to his companion, laid his head on her shoulder, and wept. She waited patiently until he was done and repeated:

"I need you … we all do".

At that she led him to his own sun-drenched bower overlooking the courtyard. There on a side table was a bowl of warm water on which floated rose petals, and he succumbed like a child to having his face, hands and then feet bathed in the fragrant liquid. After that, he was bought grapes and honey cake – the most delicious he had ever tasted. This he washed down with cool elderflower-scented water, and when he had had his fill, he was encouraged to lie down on the cushioned bench where he soon fell into a deep sleep.

In the days that followed, the routine was unvaried. He would wake from his bench when the sun was already flooding through the courtyard. His companion would join him and as he breakfasted on fruit and scented tea, she would begin her incantation.

"I need you…we all do. You are needed."

It was so gently offered that it was no more intrusive than the rustle of leaves in the trees or the soft lapping of the fountain. Around the courtyard others were stirring and, joined by their companions, would begin a slow circling of the cloister.

The day would pass in this fashion with frequent breaks for refreshment and rest. As dusk fell, each pair would return to their bower; then, as soon as their charges fell asleep, the companions would slip away until morning.

At no point would other words, explanations or instructions be offered and he, in his contentment, would ask for none.

"The healing sun, the healing sun…warming the stone." The words echoed in his head and he felt well.

And then towards the close of another perfect day, it occurred to him to offer something of his own; to give something back. He turned to look at his companion and squeezing her hand, said

"I need you."

She smiled for a few seconds and, encouraged, he said again:

"I need you…we all do."

This time she began to laugh, gently at first and then jubilantly and unrestrained. Her eyes glistened with tears of joy or sadness – he could not tell. But the laughter had caught hold of him as well and it seemed as if they could not stop. When it seemed as though they might, he repeated the words that had set them off and they began again. Others in the cloister had turned to watch them, smiling indulgently and some giving silent applause.

Eventually they quieted and arm in arm they returned to his bench as dusk approached. Tired now, he lay on his cushions and was soon asleep.

When he woke the next morning, the cloister was grey and he was quite alone. As he emerged from his bower, he felt cold rain on his face and he knew that his time in this place was at an end. He felt a momentary resurgence of his old despair but, as if anticipating this moment, a familiar voice echoed through the cloister.

"We need you … we all do."

She was not there of course, but it was enough to give him heart. Turning up the collar of his coat he turned and walked purposefully into the passageway through which they had come, how many days ago?

He strode up the ramp and as he turned each corner, the shadows deepened once more. But he felt – he hated the word, but it was apt enough – *empowered*. Within a few minutes he found himself again in the basement level of the mall. It took a moment to adjust to the gloom but he could just make out the pool of light from the floor above and made towards it, anxious to regain the street.

Again he encountered the homeless, sleeping in doorways. To the first he said:

" I need you my friend – we all do."

"Fuck off," came the reply.

Undaunted he moved on the next.

"I need you friend – we all…"

The old man sat up abruptly.

"Thanks mate – I certainly need you. Got any change?"

"No…I…I'm sorry."

The man sank back down and pulled his filthy blanket over his head.

The next didn't move but from the one after that he drew a more encouraging response. A woman held up a bottle in acknowledgement and gave him a wide toothless smile.

Encouraged, he made his way back to the foot of the broken escalator and prepared to re-enter the world outside. As he ascended, two teenage boys appeared at the top and began to make their way downwards. They looked like they had been up all night – for several nights at that. Both had skin the colour of tripe and, though unshaven, could manage only dirty smudges of beard. Both were huddled into thin hooded tops, hands stuffed into their pockets. There was a strange jerkiness to their movements as they came face to face with him. In other circumstances he would have taken the precaution of turning round and keeping well out of their way but, today, he was a different him.

"I need you – we all…"

The face of the first boy came rapidly towards him and he misread it, thinking it the beginning of an embrace. When the head-butt smashed into his nose, he still had not quite understood. Reeling, he repeated his mantra.

"I need…" but he got no further.

The second boy had withdrawn his hand from his pocket

and thrust it towards him. The blade sliced sweetly between his ribs. He felt no pain – just confusion.

"…we all do," he whispered and then tumbled as if in slow motion to the bottom of the escalator.

The boys clattered on down, kicking out in disgust as they stepped over him.

"Fuckin' weirdo."

ADDUCTION

"Last call for Royal Air Maroc flight 8463 to Tangiers. Last call for Royal Air Maroc flight 8463 to Tangiers." The tannoyed voice echoed across the sparsely peopled departure lounge. That early in the morning and on a non-holiday weekend, there were relatively few flights leaving and it was probable that all who needed to know were comfortably settled on board.

The staff at the departure gate consulted their lists and, shortly after, a further message echoed through the lounge.

"Last call for Mrs and Miss Bennet. Your flight 8463 to Tangiers is now boarding."

With no response evident, their next task was to alert security – standard procedure when luggage had been checked in but there was no sign of the passenger. But before they could make the call, they heard voices that, in the early morning hush, were difficult to ignore: angry voices, accompanied by the grind of wheelies and the clacking of heels on the hardwood floor.

Scurrying towards them were the Bennets, mother and daughter. The mother was sturdily built and dressed in a way that was unmistakably that of a British middle-aged woman indifferent to fashion: a loose-fitting floral-patterned frock, topped by a brass-buttoned shortie blazer open at the front. On her head she wore a wide-brimmed hat with a ribbon spilling down the back. She displayed bare legs and sensible lace-up suede shoes. Her expression was a combination of sad defeat and frustration.

The cause of the frustration trailed behind her. Bennet junior, a girl in her mid-teens, having made good use of the concession outlets, and clutching a number of bags in addition to her wheely, followed sullenly on.

This was Phoebe, fifteen years old and as sturdy as her mother. Her dedication to appearance, though, stood in stark contrast to her mother's indifference. Heavily made-up, with a preference for white foundation and kholed eyes, her concept of travel wear consisted of a tight-fitting black riding jacket, and a pair of low-waisted denim shorts from which emerged robust legs clad in black diamond-pattern tights. On her feet were a pair of ankle-length patent leather, high heeled boots.

"…as fast as I can *mother*. It's not my fault we're late. Stop being annoying. I didn't want to come anyway."

"Don't start that again darling. I'm doing this for you and for him. It's only fair."

"Don't give me that fair thing. It's just for you, innit?"

"Innit, innit, innit. What on earth does that mean? You'll have to talk properly when you get there. Your father won't understand a word you're saying. He's a very educated man you know."

"Yeah, yeah, so you keep telling me. Whatever…"

By this time they had arrived at the boarding gate and the staff, having resumed their positions, took a look at their passes and then went into a Keystone panic of activity. The two women were rushed through the gantry in the last moments before it was due to be wheeled away.

A stewardess did her best to settle them quickly into their seats, a procedure that involved them stumbling past a lone passenger sitting in the aisle seat – a be-suited, red-faced, nervously sweating man, who was clearly not looking forward to take-off.

"I want to sit by the window," said Phoebe.

"That's where I always like to sit – what difference does it make to you … ?" said her mother.

"I just want to sit there, OK? For Christ's s … "

Noticing that their spat wasn't helping their neighbour's nerves, Phoebe's mum attempted conciliation.

"I'm sorry dear, we're a bit discombobulated. Our taxi didn't arrive on time. We'll sort out our seating arrangements once we're in flight. Now for goodnesss sake Phoebe, just sit down. We'll sort it out later."

The plane took off, and once Phoebe had achieved her aim of bagging the window seat, the rest of the four-hour flight should have passed without incident. Phoebe, though, did not want to be on the plane and expressed her discontent any way she could. She was quick to free herself from her seat belt, and then made it her business to explore every one of the facilities available. Her overhead light was switched and swivelled repeatedly, her seat tray was banged up and down, much to the annoyance of the passengers in front. The passengers behind had to endure her experiments with the recline lever and, indeed, tolerate her choice of maximum recline for the duration of the flight. Maddingly, she sang along to her ipod in a tuneless dirge and when asked to stop by a neighbour responded wth sullen scowls and no more was said.

Her first complaint to the stewardess came no more than five minutes into the flight. "There's something wrong with this screen. Like, I'm not getting the movie."

"That's because we haven't started it yet," replied the stewardess archly.

"Whatever," was the inevitable response.

Lunch, when it came, was a nightmare for the staff. She complained three times: the food was cold, she had ordered the vegan option whatever the records said, why was her pudding smaller than everyone else's?

The airline had promised free alcoholic drinks, but of course just for adults, and Phoebe was not happy about that. The fact that her mother did not take up the option was of scant compensation. She expressed her dissatisfaction by demanding a succession of soft drinks from the increasingly frazzled cabin staff.

"Think of it as a preparation Phoebe, you won't have any opportunity to drink when we get there. "

"What do you mean, I won't get any opportunity?"

"Well, they're Muslim aren't they? They don't drink as far as I know.'

"Oh great, now you tell me. Like I told you I didn't want to come. Why are you doing this to me?"

Their voices had become increasingly loud as the passengers around them were treated to a full-blown row. Phoebe thrust her face at her mother, angrier than ever.

"Why won't you ever listen to me? I told you I wasn't interested in seeing him. Like if he cared so much, how come he never came back to visit?"

"It was me Phoebe. It was *me* that kept you from seeing *him*. You hear such stories you know, especially from those types of places. The men think they own everything. Surely you've heard of abduction … you know fathers stealing their children. I wasn't going to risk it Phoebe. I wasn't having you locked up in some kind of harem being bullied by his mother, and when you were barely old enough being married off to some old man that you'd never even met."

"What? You think I'd put up with anyone – *anyone* – telling me what I can and can't do. Like how long've you known me … ?"

"That's not the point Phoebe. You were very young. They would have moulded you. Bent you to their will. You know what those countries are like. Anyway, what about me? You were mine, you were my little girl. Gorgeous you were … my little angel I used to call you."

"Oh yuk, don't make me throw up. Anyway, if you care so much, like why are we seeing him now? I mean its not like I can remember him. This is for you innit? Still fancy him do you? Oh god, you do don't you? At your age. It's disgusting."

"No Phoebs, you've got it wrong."He wasn't a bad man. It was his family I was worried about. I mean the man is God and all that sort of attitude. He has all the rights. But things've changed since those days. They've got more like us – you know what with the internet and things. He's been in touch over the years. Always asking about you. He wanted to see you – I mean family is very important to them. It's only fair isn't it, even if it's just the once? Anyway, like you say, you can handle yourself now. You won't put up with any nonsense."

"Too right, and like I'm not wearing a headscarf neither.

Looks well minging."

"Oh Phoebe, just try and make the best of it. It'll be interesting – I mean apart from Torremolinos when you were
small, we've never really been abroad. Think of it: deserts,
camels, palm trees, exotic food and things. Please try and …
behave nicely."

"Like I don't have much choice do I – and I'm not eating
their rubbish food neither."

Phoebe's string of drinks had their inevitable consequence
and she made frequent visits to the toilet. During her occupa-
tions, significant queues would form as the quarter hours
ticked by. Each time she would reappear with newly thickened
layers of make-up, something of a shock to those waiting next
in line.

Passengers would later dine out on stories of their flight
from hell. The nervous neighbour, once comfortably back on
the ground, amused his companions with the conceit that, as
the row between mother and daughter reached a crescendo,
he of all people had begun praying for the plane to crash.

At last it was over, and passengers disembarked with noticeable alacrity into the heat and blinding light of Tangier Ibn
Battouta Airport.

Phoebe was quick to take offence. Her chosen outfit attracted more attention than even she would have wished and she
realised that the chorus of wolf whistles and shouts that accompanied their exit from the terminal was less to do with appreciation and more to do with ridicule or even anger. The
heat, too, she took as a personal attack on her right to comfort.

"For god's sake, I can't breathe. How do people live like … "

She broke off at the sight of a group of people moving towards her. Leading them, arms outstretched in greeting, was a corpulent middle-aged man in a business suit. His concession to the heat was the open neck-shirt and bare, sandaled feet. A glance at the gold glinting at wrist and neck told of his affluence. This, she assumed, was her father Jimol. Behind him were four females.

The first, a short ball-shaped woman was dressed in a black burqa from which unfriendly eyes stared hard at them. OMG that's my gran!, thought Phoebe. Next was a burly looking woman in a drab djellaba and headscarf. Her expression was disdainful and fully open to view. Stepmother!

Tottering behind her in high heels were two girls, just a bit younger than Phoebe, who were consulting their phones rather than paying much attention. Wearing modest knee-length blouses over their tight jeans, they were, nevertheless, a riot of colour. True, they too wore headscarves, but atop those were glitzy wraparound sunglasses.

"Lillian, Phoebe how good to see you," boomed the man. He reached out to the former and pumped her hands in greeting before touching his hand respectfully to his heart. His mother and wife looked on sourly. Then it was Phoebe's turn and with rather less reserve he grabbed her by the shoulders and kissed her six times on alternate cheeks, causing her to recoil from his sweaty tobacco-scented embrace. Undaunted he gestured expansively to his women folk.

"Allow me to present my mother and my wife Sulayma." The two women made no attempt to touch them but nodded briefly and disapprovingly in their direction.

"And now Phoebe, let me introduce you to your half-sisters,

Yasmin and Kamar."

"Hi," said one.

"Hi," said the other.

Neither had lifted their eyes from their phones.

Phoebe knew just what to do. She stared down at her own phone. "Yeah – whatever," she muttered.

"The car is not far," said her father. "It will take us all. We can go back to my house for lunch and then get you over to your hotel later. What do you say?"

"Oh that's nice of you Jimol, but I had another thought, said Phoebe's mother "The main thing is you two need to get to know each other. You must have lots to talk about. I'll tell you what – why don't I explore the town for an hour or so? I could visit the souk – I've always wanted to go to a souk. Then I'll meet you back at our hotel and we'll decide what to do this evening and plan the rest of the week."

"Well at least let one of the girls show you around Lillian. It can be a bit bewildering for foreigners…"

"No really, I'll be fine. You take Phoebe and the luggage and we'll catch up later."

Phoebe eyed her mother imploringly.

"Muuum…" she began.

"No Phoebe, its okay, I'll be fine on my own," she said, wilfully misunderstanding.

"That's fine Lillian," said Jimol. My family are absolutely thrilled that you have come and can't wait to meet the two of you after all these years. We've planned a big celebration you know. We'll tell you all about it tonight. Enjoy your afternoon."

With that he put a fat arm around Phoebe and began to lead

her away in the direction of the car park. She threw a sullen parting look at her mother before giving way.

Lillian stood for some time watching them, her hand shading her eyes from the bright sun. Each time Phoebe threw a resentful look back over her shoulder, she gave a little wave of encouragement. At last they disappeared from view.

A casual observer might assume that the drab English woman, standing stock still on the concourse, was in some kind of trouble; transfixed by sadness perhaps?

Five minutes passed, then ten. Two stewardesses stopped for a moment and were about to approach her to offer help but at that moment she seemed to snap out of her reverie and they went on their way.

She began to rummage around in her shoulder bag, walking as she did so towards a litter bin. Smiling a slow quiet smile, she withdrew two passports. After inspecting them carefully, she selected one and, snapping it shut, threw it in the bin. She looked at it for a moment and then, reaching in, pushed it deep below the top layers. The other she returned to her bag.

Next, she pulled out two airline tickets and, having carefully selected one, ripped it into pieces, which she also consigned to the bin.

Clutching the remaining ticket and passport, she re-entered the terminal and took an escalator to the departure level, alighting with a noticeable spring in her step as an announcement rang out: "Passengers for Royal Air Maroc flight 3648 to London should now proceed to check in."

MIDNIGHT RAMBLER

"Come on mother, for god's sake. Mother!"

Gordon leant over the huddled form of Marjorie, his 82-year-old mother who, having gone to bed at nine o'clock the previous evening, was, at noon the following day, still apparently asleep. Her face was turned away from him and the bedclothes were pulled resolutely around her ears.

Noticing that her hearing aids were on her bedside table, he raised his voice to a shout: "We're having lunch in half an hour. Now please get up and, just for once, join us. Mother!"

She turned to face him, opened one eye and gave him a sweet smile "Okay dear, I'll get up in a minute. No need to shout."As he left her room, she turned back to the wall, pulled her duvet more securely about her and with a smile playing about her mouth, drifted back to the vivid dream she had been having.

With lunch on the table, and his wife plonking the plates down on the table with unmistakeable peevishness, Gordon pondered his dilemma. There was, essentially, nothing physically or mentally wrong with his mother – at least not enough for her not to be able to spend the daylight hours with them. She could, if she cared sufficiently, even look after the kids from time to time and give them a break. Isabelle and Rory, eight and ten, were a hyperactive twosome, always on the go.

When they weren't concocting elaborate games involving a good deal of mess and rearranged furniture, they were involved in bitter, long-lasting arguments. Frankly they were exhausting.

The problem was his wife, Naomi, a relentlessly driven person who tried to bring the same skills she so successfully applied as an NHS administrator to matters of household and family. Gordon found *her* exhausting too.

To be honest, he thought, if the old woman chose to sleep her life away, then let her. At least she was safe in her bed and no bother to him. She had, in her own words, 'had enough'. She would look at him in a way that made him feel she was making fun of him and say, "You don't understand. I'm old me. You'll be like this one day." And with that she would turn back to the wall, wriggle in exaggerated pleasure and sink back to sleep with a mischievous smile playing on her lips. This had been going on ever since she had moved in with them eighteen months previously. It was not unusual for her to sleep twenty hours of the twenty-four.

She hadn't left the house in months and only then when they had insisted that she drive with them to the gardens at Walmer Castle to admire the first flowers of spring. It had not been a success. She had slept on the way there, insisted that they leave her in the tea room while they did the tour ("Not on these legs dear. I'm old me"), and then slept all the way back.

Naomi's irritation with the old woman was exacerbated by the pride she had about her own father. Aged 87, he lived independently and was still capable of striding into town each day to sink a pint or so with friends. He went to the cinema and the theatre and read voraciously. She suspected, too, that there was a woman in his life and took some delight in that thought. Needless to say, his waking hours failed to coincide with those of Gordon's mother, and the two had never met.

Naomi's mood had not improved with Marjorie's non-appearance and, as she noisily cleared away the old woman's uneaten lunch, she launched into a familiar tirade. "I've had enough of this. She treats us like we don't exist. She's perfectly capable of helping out – with the cooking, with the kids. I'm just her skivvy. When are you going to say something? She walks all over you – or she would if she ever got out of bed."

"What do you expect me to do? I can't force her to get up. Shall I tip the bed up? Tip her on the floor? What do you want me to do? And I have talked to her, but do you know what she said to me? 'I just want to have a good sleep and then one day "wake up dead". '

'That is so pathetic," snapped back Naomi. "There is absolutely nothing wrong with her."

"I know, I know. Sometimes I think she's just mocking us. Taking the piss."

In the heat of the exchange he'd forgotten that the children were still at the table. They, though, were intent on reminding him. "You swore dad, you swore," chortled Isabelle. 'Taking the piss, taking the piss," echoed her brother, and the two of them collapsed into shrieks of laughter.

"Oh god," said their mother, hands over her ears. "This is doing my head in. I've had just about enough."

Things settled down a little for the afternoon. Gordon tried to watch rugby, Naomi tried to read her book but both found it impossible to give these activities their full attention. The situation was not helped by the children, who, having looked like cooperating over a puzzle, soon embarked on another monumental squabble.

Fortunately, a Saturday afternoon family ritual was about to take place: tea and a home-made cake. That day's was a corker: an apple and ginger sponge with a maple syrup and cream cheese topping. Just for a moment, the hubbub subsided and they all gathered in front of the newly-lit open fire in the sitting room As Gordon started slicing, he mentally counted the seconds before there would be a creaking from the corridor and his mother's face would appear round the door having, just by chance, got up to visit the bathroom. He counted to twenty before she appeared. About par, he thought.

"Oh, tea – have you got enough for an extra cup? My, that cake looks good – could I try a teensy slice?"

Space was found for her in front of the fire. One of the children was sent to fetch the dressing gown from her bedroom to put round her shoulders and the scene was, for all the world, that of a happy family.

During these interludes Marj was more than capable of playing her part. The children loved the twinkly old woman with her slightly batty manner and cheeky demean. As she munched her way through two huge chunks of cake and swilled three cups of tea, she cuddled one child then the other, asking them questions about their friends and schools.

After half an hour though, she went through a familiar routine. Running the back of her hand over her forehead and yawning dramatically she said, "Ooh I'm tired me. Granny's old you know. She needs another nap." And then she hauled herself laboriously back onto her feet before shuffling her way down the corridor and back to bed.

"Even if she appears for dinner, I reckon today will be a record sleep-in," said Naomi. "It can't be good for her and its bloody frustrating."

"Ooh mum sweared," chanted Rory

"Shut up," snapped his mother.

"Don't take it out on the kids," said Gordon.

"I don't think I can take this any more," his wife replied. "I don't know about anyone else. I mean after all we do for her, you'd think she could give something back – at least spend some time with the children. It's exhausting this – I mean we spend so much energy rowing about it, trying to get her on her feet, trying to get her into her day clothes, trying to get her out of the house once in a while. I'm beginning to hate her. I know that's an awful thing to say but that's the way I feel."

There was a moment of hope at dinnertime when they heard approaching steps just as they were about to eat.

"Come on mother," Gordon called, "we've laid a place for you." There was no reply but the sound of the bathroom door closing.

"Well, hopefully she's having a shower," said Naomi, "and not before time – she was a bit wiffy earlier."

Again, the children found this irresistibly hilarious. "Wiffy, wiffy," they choused.

After ten minutes, as they tackled dessert, the creeking approached and Marj poked her nose almost shyly round the door, her head swathed in a towel.

"I've just had a shower loves, it's made me proper tired –

can you bring me a little something to eat in bed."

"No we can't Marjorie, if you want to eat – sit down and eat with your family," snapped Naomi, with rather more vehemence than she had intended.

Marj turned away: "If that's your attitude, I'll do without," and off she went, creak, creak down the corridor.

"Oh for Christ's sake," said Gordon. "I'll take her some."

"You always do this don't you – make excuses, indulge her. How is she ever going to change her behaviour?"

"Look, she's my mother for god's sake. What do you want me to do, chuck her out?"

"Great idea – why don't you?"

The row sea-sawed back and forth for the best part of an hour until they ran out of invective and slumped into a state of bitter exhaustion. The children had slunk off to bed of their own accord, the heat of the argument alarming even them.

It was not yet eleven when they turned in. The strain of the day and the arguing having taken its toll, they collapsed into bed, now not speaking to each other and both more than willing to find relief in sleep.

Midnight. The only sound, apart from the ticking of the mantelpiece clock, was of a car engine gently turning over in the street outside. Marj pulled the sheet down from her face and listened intently before slipping out of bed. She crept over to the massive dark-wood wardrobe to the left of the door. It was a piece of her own furniture, predictably hated by Gordon and Naomi. It was deep and capacious. There were two drawers below and then, in the upper cupboard, was a rail on which hung a selection of 'old lady' garments, mostly protected with plastic covers and smelling of naphthalene.

At the back of the wardrobe, and hidden by the clothes, was a built-in rectangular compartment. Marj reached in and lifting the hinged lid as quietly as possible, brought out an item wrapped neatly in brown paper. Unfolding it on her bed she stepped back in renewed admiration as the crimson silk dress came into view. Next out of the box was a pair of black tights and a pair of high-heeled shoes encrusted with silver glitter.

Before long she was dressed in all these things and admiring herself in the wardrobe mirror. She paused for a moment and approached the window. There she held up five fingers before producing some lipstick and mascara from the washing bag by her bed.

The lipstick matched exactly the red of her dress and the kohl against the blue of her eyes gave her, she thought, a touch of the Liz Taylor's. After a squirt of perfume and some vigorous hair brushing, there were just two more items to complete the look. These she had no need to hide away, being appropriate for her age and station. Now, though, they were put to stylish use.

First was the long string of pearls that she had inherited from her own mother. Looped twice around her neck, they formed a dazzling choker, with the added bonus that they covered the wrinklier bits of her neck. Next, the ancient fox fur that, while it admittedly smelt a bit mangy, looked fabulous slung casually about her shoulders.

Satisfied now, she crept, shoes in hand, to the front door and quietly let herself out.

"Hey Ted," she called as she emerged from the entrance lobby.

"Hey gorgeous," replied Ted, "Where to tonight girl?"

"Let's kick off at Boodgies."

"You sure girl – it can get pretty hyper this time of night."

"Perfect," said Marj and climbed into the passenger seat.

Boodgies was a hybrid sort of place. Down on the bleak road that ran past the waterfront, it had for many years, then as the Hope and Anchor, been the pub of choice for hard-drinking dockers and sailors. In an era when pubs closed at eleven, it had been famous for the length and frequency of its lock-ins, not to mention the use that its upstairs rooms were put to. At intervals during the evening, pale-faced women would appear at the door to one side of the main bar and another punter would drain his drink and disappear upstairs.

Then it developed a reputation for hosting aspiring bands, some of which had gone on to national acclaim. This in turn changed the balance of the clientele. Many more youngsters adopted the place, hoping to be part of whatever new thing was happening and, in truth, excited too by its wild reputation, now extending to the quality of dope to be found there. The good old boys still drank there, albeit as part of the scenery. Respectable it was not.

She knew how to make an entrance. Ted held open the door to the main bar and she sashayed in as though she was on a catwalk. The place was packed but all heads turned and a cheer went up from young and old alike. The band, noodling away on a long guitar solo, stopped playing and raised the necks of their guitars in acknowledgement. They knew the form. One of them skipped over to the vintage juke box in the corner and pressed a few buttons. Little old Lady from

Pasadena was the choice. A hundred voices joined in with the Beach Boys when they got to the refrain: 'Go granny, go granny, go granny, go'. It echoed down the street, round the misty dockyard and beyond.

Marj took immediately to the dance floor and twirled like a dervish. Everyone looked on with admiration and then spilled out to join her with much whooping and waving of hands in the air.

Ted had work to do and left her with people jostling to buy her a drink. "Be back in an hour or so doll. Enjoy yourself," he called over his shoulder.

When he returned it was approaching two and Marj looked like she had indeed enjoyed herself. He found her sitting on the lap of one of the old seadogs, a scoundrel called Nathaniel. He had clearly just finished one of his notoriously filthy stories and Marj was shrieking with ear-splitting laughter and lightly slapping him round the face with her fox fur, in mock disapproval.

"All right gal?" said Ted. "Home now?"

"Fffuck no Ted," slurred Marjorie. "My young friends're just off to Sch…Sch…Schizo Nite at'er Empori…rium…'ve asked me t'go wivem."

"OK love, gett'em together and I'll get you all over there, but just for an hour mind and then it's home to beddy-byes."

The friends, two boys and a girl, were gathered together. Compared to 'Liz Taylor' they looked unlikely companions. The boys were all assymetric hair, spray-on jeans and moody expressions. The girl, three sheets to the wind, was dressed only in a tiny halter top and bum-revealing shorts. Ted was at a loss to understand what they saw in Marj until she paused for a second over a manhole cover on the pavement. It didn't blow her skirt up but it fanned out as she gave a twirl. That's it, thought Ted – 'Marylin' – retro credibility.

The Emporium was pumping. It was possible to stand outside on the pavement and still feel the percussive effects of heavy bass. Marj and her mates approached the thuggish looking doormen. Spotting her they broke into wide smiles and stood aside to let them in. "Evenin' Marji – lookin' good girl. Take it easy now, s'mental in there."

"One hour girl," said Ted as she disappeared from view. Then he leant in to speak to one of the bouncers: "Keep an eye on her Jimbo, She's'ad quite a lot. Don't mind about annuver glass or two but if you see any pills do'in the rounds, keep 'em away from 'er. She'd scoff the lot given the chance." The two men laughed conspiratorially.

"No worries Ted – we'll see her right. I'll tell the boys inside."

He was back at three thirty just as the sky had begun to lighten. The bouncers had been true to their word and had Marj ready and waiting just inside the entrance, out of the morning chill. She looked more than happy with her night and, a little unsteadily, was twirling around to some remembered waltz tune playing only in her head. Ted placed his jacket round her shoulders and led her over to the cab.

They didn't leave immediately as Ted reached for his vacuum flask in a well-practised routine. "'ere we are girl – the usual," and he waited patiently as she sipped at the strong, sweet coffee.

Back at the flats, he waited in the cab as Marj approached the entry door. She quickly punched in the code and disappeared from view.

Managing to enter the flat without a sound having removed her shoes outside the door, she then closed it equally deftly behind her. Then she went into the bathroom and gave a quick wave from the window. Ted, watching for it, knew that was his signal to return to his own bed.

Regaining the corridor, she became aware instantly that she was not alone. There, in the gloom, a fearful pair of eyes watched this exotic apparition coming towards him.

It was a toss up who was the more surprised and both stood momentarily paralysed. Rory, finally recognising his grandmother, was the first to react. He gave a hesitant smile and then started towards her. "Gran…"

Marj raised a finger to her lips and, smiling, whispered, "Shhhh Rory boy. Our secret OK?"

The boy nodded and the two of them made their way back to their respective bedrooms, the early dawn light throwing long shadows down the length of the corridor.

THE STRAWBERRY PEOPLE

"So tell me about this guy – how'd ya know him?" asked Steve of his friend.

River thought for a moment and replied, "We were in high school together. Even then he was a bit special, kinda cooler than anyone around. It was like an aura – like he knew more'n the rest of us. Even the teachers felt it and used to defer to him. And the chicks man – could've had any one he wanted but I can only remember the one. She was like him – you know – head in the clouds. They seemed untouchable. We all started college together – they were majoring in Philosophy but dropped out after one semester. That's when I lost contact. Mind you I heard stuff every now and then. That he'd set up a wholefood store here with his girlfriend – what's her name? Nothin' much came of it apparently. Barely lasted six months I hear tell. It was before its time – way before people even knew what wholefood was. They got called cranks, crazies, hippy bums. Most folks were more'n happy to eat cheap supermarket shit. Anyways I guess this is where we make a start. The shop should be round here somewhere."

River, a gangly saturnine six-footer, and his friend Steve – a chunky, cheery blond with the build of a quarter back – had been on the Buckeye Trail for two weeks. More weekend hikers than hobos and travelling with light packs, they had chosen a route that offered accommodation and meals in the small towns that were on or near that part of the Ohio trail. It hadn't stopped them dressing the part. Both wore fringed frontiersmen jackets, River with a wide-brimmed leather stetson and Steve with a bandana worn low on his forehead. By then they were fetchingly dusty, had picked up convincing tans from their days in the sun and were beginning to see themselves as kings of the road, disciples of Woody.

City boys both, they had nevertheless chosen the trail hike for their annual vacation and had taken this diversion to satisfy River's curiosity about his old school friend. The dusty little town of Boulder Creek was where he'd last heard of him and his shop.

Boulder Creek was just a handful of concrete buildings, having no discernible reason for existing apart from servicing the single-lane blacktop that ran through it. There they found the shop, or what was left of it. A peeling wood sign hanging half-off above the window bore the legend: 'Whole Food Organics'. Peering through the cobwebbed window they could just make out a dingy room in which were the remains of sacks of grain and mouldering boxes on collapsing shelves. As their sight adjusted they saw that the floor was covered with rat droppings and, for that matter, several dried-out corpses of those responsible. Fallen to the bottom of the window was a yellowing notice: 'Closed until further notice'.

"Wow, I wasn't expecting this," said River. "I mean..." He wasn't sure what he meant but instead of finishing his sentence, he threw his weight against the door, which showed no sign of giving way.

"Here let me," said Steve reckoning on his additional 20 pounds being more up to the task.

They were being watched though, and before Steve could make his run, a young woman holding a baby in her arms crossed the dusty street towards them. She can't be any older than us, thought River, but she had a hollow-eyed, exhausted look that reminded him of the pictures he'd seen of itinerant women in dust bowl days.

"Ain't no one here no more," she drawled quietly as if the effort of speaking was too much.

"Yeah, we can see that. They were old friends of ours – where'd they go?"

"Up country a piece – two, three years gone. Real old-style heads, don't have nothing to do with no one – grow all their own food and stuff."

River had gone silent and was staring hard at the woman. "Rosa?"

"Yeah s'my name – who're you?"

"Rosa it's me, River – remember – high school? What happened Rosa – to the shop – and Dave? Where's Dave?"

She looked at him blankly for a moment and then her eyes widened with recognition.

"Yeah, I got it – River. You were quite tight to us for a while right?" She paused and looked at the ground as though needing a moment to process the memory. Then she continued:"It's like I'm saying, they took off up country, Dave and all. Got themselves a commune – like it's the 70s or somethin'. It got too weird for me. I stayed behind but Dave was deep in. He became some sort of guru figure. They dig all this new age stuff but the weirdest thing is that they worship the strawberry. I ain't kidding. That's what I hear. They grow 'em year after year but they ain't allowed to eat them. Just watch the beauties rot away in front of their eyes. Seems like a terrible waste to me but that's what I hear. The denial is supposed to encourage spiritual growth. I mean Dave, or whatever he calls himself now, sets the rules."

"That's one helluva rule," whistled Steve "Where do we find them? I mean, is it okay to drop by?"

"I guess, but my advice would be to leave them be like most folks around here do. I've heard they don't take too kindly to strangers."

"All the same," said River, "sounds kinda interesting and after all I'm not entirely a stranger."

"Well, no stranger'n he is," said Rosa smiling for the first time. "If you really want to find them, follow this road along to the edge of town. There's a store there. You'll need to take water and food. You head out east on a rough trail that cuts away from the road half a mile on. Then you got yourselves a ten-mile hike into deep country. After that I don't know – somewheres around there."

At the store they made their purchases and in response to the owner's curiosity about their impending trip, told him of what they were planning to do. It seemed he too knew of the commune:

"Yeah we know they're out there. Don't bother us none though. Keep themselves to themselves. South-east of here, ten, maybe twelve, miles. Cousin of mine ran across them a few years ago. He was out hunting that way and saw them out in their goddam strawberry fields. He started over to wish them the best of the day but they began shouting and making it pretty damn clear he should keep his distance. Didn't bother him none. Excuse me gentlemen but 'Fuck em' were his actual words. I'd be careful out there. I hear tell that the county law boys been nosin' around. Gonna move them on or somethin'. Seems they don't actually own the land out that way. Leave 'em be, that's what I say. Ain't hurting no one."

Having stocked up with food and water enough for two days, the two men trudged off to find the trail. For the first few miles and still within earshot of the road, they passed through a flat landscape that showed signs of once having been cultivated. Now it had degenerated into dust-whorled scrub. Further on, the path began to rise a little and on the brow of a hill still a mile or two ahead they caught their first glimpse of dense forest, a hazy blue in the midday light. An hour on and they passed into the deep shadow that the forest offered. The temperature dropped as they did so and the only sound they were aware of was the snapping of twigs beneath their feet.

By late afternoon they had begun to doubt the wisdom of the trip. They had encountered no sign or clue as to the whereabouts of the strawberry people. The unchanging path plunged on and on through the ever-cooling forest. At last they came to a small glade with a clear water stream running through it and, unconfident of reaching any kind of shelter that night, topped up their water bottles as a precaution.

Twenty minutes later they encountered a fork in the path and, in the absence of any pertinent information and tired of walking endlessly ahead, chose the left at random. It was a decision that within minutes paid dividends.

They emerged into a massive clearing. So sudden was the transition from deeply-shaded path to glaring sun that it took a moment for their eyes to adjust. There in front of them was an open field of tilled reddish soil striated with lines of bright green low bushes dotted with red fruit – the fabled strawberries.

At first glance there seemed to be dull humps at intervals along the lines. These it transpired were pickers – all women – bent to their task. They were dressed uniformly in drab ankle-length skirts with long-sleeved blouses. Most wore pioneer-style bonnets against the heat of the sun.

"Wow" said Steve "This has got to be them, let's go talk to them."

They moved towards the nearest picker, who looked up at the friends with alarm on her face. Before either could speak they felt heavy hands on their shoulders. Spinning round, they came face-to-face with a couple of men. Both were substantial in build. Dressed like hippies, they were nonetheless unsmiling and aggressive in manner. Instinctively River and Steve began to communicate in what they hoped was the appropriate patois:

"Hey, peace man, how ya doin'? What's goin' down fellas – we near the strawberry folk? We lookin' for a guy called … "

"Who sent you boys? You got no business here. Best you turn around and go straight back to where you come from. You hear me." The speaker pushed his chest aggressively against them as he spoke, attempting to nudge them round and away from the sight of the women.

"No man, you don't understand. I'm an old buddy of Dave's. Word is he set up this here commune."

"Ain't no one here with that name boy. You wrong – now I suggest you move yo' asses outa here." At that point his companion pulled him to one side and out of the immediate hearing of the friends conducted a mumbled conversation, after which he turned back to them.

"Seems my colleague here thinks he knows who you mean – Dave who used to run the store back in Boulder Creek?"

"Yeah man, that's him."

"Well he ain't called Dave no more and you'd best not try. He's Brother now."

"Well, can we just say hi to brother Dave?"

"Just *Brother*, asshole. He the main man round here – not sure if he'll see you or no. You hip to his teachings?"

"Teachings? Well no but…"

Before he could finish his sentence, the friends were grabbed by their shoulders and marched away from the strawberry field, back to the fork where they'd made their diversion. This time they were guided onto the right hand fork. After five minutes they came to another clearing filled with a drab collection of dwellings, tepees, shacks, trailers.

The few adults and children they encountered as they entered the encampment seemed uninterested in the strangers. All walked with heads down as though in deep contemplation. The absence of bright colour continued in their clothing and, for that matter, in their ashen faces and dull eyes.

Any younger child that couldn't resist staring at the colourful strangers were instantly corrected by the adults and forced to look away. Steve leaned in to River and whispered, "Sheez man, ain't seen heads like these before – look like the livin' dead to my eyes."

Against that dull background though, they couldn't fail to notice frequent flashes of colour like beacons guiding their way through the encampment. On top of posts driven into the ground or on stone cairns were silver bowls each piled high with gleaming red strawberries.

Soon they came to a brown canvas-patched pavilion tent into which they were roughly pushed. "Wait there fellas – we'll see if Brother will see you – whadya say your names were?"

"River McCorkdale, he'll remember me from high school and this is my buddy Steve Farsides."

"Okay. Just wait here and don't go talkin' to no one. One more thing," – he indicated a bowl of strawberries standing on a crate in the centre of the otherwise empty tent. Illuminated by a shaft of light coming through a central ventilation hole in the roof, the colour seemed to bleed into the surrounding gloom. "We don't – you don't, ever eat those babies. Don't even think 'bout it. One day we will. Brother will say when. Meanwhile resist and save yo' sorry asses from temptation."

Having issued the warning, the two could be heard laughing mockingly as they strode off, leaving the two friends bewildered by the turn of events. After a couple of minutes, Steve, always the more rebellious of the two, moved towards the dish of strawberries. "Shit man, I don't care what they say, I'm ravenous," and he took a handful. Before he could eat, though, they became aware that they were not alone – peering round the tent flap and into the dim interior were two sets of pale eyes. A brother and sister, barefoot and looking like ragged hillbillies, stood staring at them.

"Steve, don't – put them back," said River, the idea that they might somehow be corrupting these kids unexpectedly entering his mind. Steve, feeling no such prick of conscience, stepped towards the waifs, waving the fruits in front of their noses. The boy, who was younger, raised his hand hesitantly to the bowl but his sister grabbed his wrist and for his benefit as well as for Steve's shook her head.

At that moment they heard the voices of their escorts returning and, as the kids ran off, Steve's bravado deserted him and he threw the fruits hurriedly back into the bowl.

"OK fellas, Brother says he'll see you. Come with us." They were led briskly into the heart of the settlement, noticing as they did so that the dwellings were in some sort of radial arrangement and that they were being led to the centre.

There was no mistaking that it was the centre. A large gleamingly white yurt stood before them, its circumference marked by fruit bowls filled, as before, with luscious red fruit.

"Shoes off fellas and leave yo' packs here – they'll be safe."

They were led through a series of flaps into a surprisingly exotic interior. The floor was carpeted with brightly-patterned carpets. Around the edges were smaller spaces curtained off from the main arena. In the very centre was a round wooden dais covered in white sheepskins. The shaft of light coming through the ventilation hole, as before, created a theatrical glow in the very centre. It was hard for the two men to be anything less than impressed by the scene before them.

On the dais, cross-legged, sat Brother in plain white robes, the light creating an aura around his head. He was a gangly, lean man and, although his face was lined and weathered by his four decades, he retained an abundant head of dark blond hair falling to his shoulders and a coarsely-trimmed beard and moustache with the stained appearance of a smoker. His eyes, a washed-out blue, showed a similar yellowing in the whites. He sat staring expressionless and motionless as the two men approached.

"Dave – sorry Brother," began River "Remember me, I..." He was silenced by a hand raised imperiously in front of them.

"Wait, there will be a time to speak but before then ..." The voice was deep and rounded, giving an impression of experience and knowledge but, thought Steve, as much to do with the evident smoking habit. Brother had turned his head to one side and clapped his hands quietly.

From one of the curtained side spaces a woman appeared holding a dish of the ubiquitous strawberries. In contrast to the drab creatures they had seen on the outside, she was dressed in a white floor- length gown, with a gold trim creating a dancing light above her bare feet. The long sleeves, tight on the arms then belling out at the wrists, were similarly trimmed. With braided blond hair held back by a headband low on her forehead and a long crimson belt loose on her hips, she looked like a pagan princess.

Brother took one of the fruits and, holding it under his nose, inhaled deeply before returning it to the dish. Then he passed a strawberry to each of the friends: "Yours to do what you will with." Feeling disorientated and uncertain, both emulated Brother, inhaling the scent before returning the fruits to the bowl.

"Welcome friends," beamed Brother. "These jewels are the gifts of the spirits of this place and we are not yet worthy of them. One day we will be ready but first there must be a time of denial, a fight against temptation, against the call of the flesh. All who abide here fight the same fight and only when the weakest of us joins hands with the strong will we, as a community, accept these earthly gifts and in doing so pass to a higher consciousness. Had you eaten the fruit, I would have judged you too corrupting to remain with us, and you would have been escorted to the perimeter. Since you have shown yourselves to be men of restraint, I say again 'welcome'. Stay awhile, talk with whom you will, listen to our message. I myself preach to the brethren each evening and would be delighted to see you there."

He signalled to one of their escorts still standing behind them. "You are free to wander where you will but it will be easier if brother Marcos is with you. He can find you somewhere to sleep and show you around our settlement – introduce you to my brothers and sisters."

With that he rose, turned away from them and, taking the arm of the handmaiden, walked across the floor and into one of the curtained-off sections.

They felt again the weight of a hand on their shoulders and were led firmly away.

Marcos, once out of the ambit of Brother, seemed to relax a little. River concluded that the signal had been given that they were not entirely unworthy guests. Still, he was disturbed by the fact that his old school friend had not asked anything about him or even showed recognition. He thought, too, that it would be useful for the community to know that the county law officials had begun to take an interest in their affairs.

They were taken to a dilapidated wooden shack, empty

except for a number of straw palliasses scattered around the single room. "Here's where you'll sleep tonight guys," said Marcos. "You'll find a water tap and a John out back. We eat in an hour, all together, and then Brother will address us – I mean all of us – brothers, sisters and children. Ain't no exceptions." Now drop your stuff here and let's go look around."

In the hour that followed, their invitation to wander round at will was anything but. Although Marcos had switched on a little friendly charm, he was careful to mediate any conversations they managed to have with individuals that he selected. As a result they heard again and again about the merits of abstinence and the rewards to come. It was explained that strawberries represented the easy sensuality and veniality of the outside world and must be resisted for spiritual health.

They heard how the season's growth was left to decompose and that from birth young children were cured of the desire for strawberries by having rotten fruit held under their noses. As a right of passage, fourteen-year-olds were smeared in rotten fruit for a week before being allowed to bathe in a stream in front of the whole community. A constant refrain was of the gratitude due to Brother who had led them to this state of grace, had kept them strong and who would guide them to the next level at a time soon to come.

They were struck again by the simple dull clothing and sickly pallor of those they met.

Marcos by contrast seemed healthy enough as had their other escort and those they'd seen in the leader's yurt. He also proved quite informative and bit by bit they were able to appreciate the workings of the commune; how their labour consisted almost entirely of growing food to sustain them. Apart from the strawberry fields, they also grew several root crops as well as cabbage, maize and oats which comprised their entire diet. Sour cooking apples provided their only permissible fruit.

Exceptions were made for Brother and those of his immediate cohort who, needing the energy to lead and guide the community, were able to supplement their diet with a range of other fruits from a restricted orchard in which chickens roamed, providing the leaders with eggs and, occasionally, meat.

They also learnt that the culture of denial extended to sexual matters. Although there were many married or other couples in the community, abstinence from sex was recommended. In order to help couples with this decision, Brother had proclaimed that all females over the age of fifteen were to be considered his wives. Although some had arrived with children ready-made, many of the new babies had been fathered by him, and the mothers, according to Marcos, felt that their children were blessed by this beneficence.

"Did you notice", said Marcos, "that Brother has the sign of grace upon him – the strawberry mark on his neck?"

"Of course," said River "I remember now, he used to be quite self-conscious about it."

"Well not now. We recognise it as the mark of the annointed. Any children that carry such a mark are specially revered."

In a moment when the friends had lagged a little behind their guide, they snatched a conversation. "River," began Steve, "What d'ya make of this? I mean its all a bit weird for me man."

"Well," replied his friend, "you say that, but there's somethin' here. Sure they look a bit raggedy, but there's a sort of ascetic vibe – plenty of precedence for that over time. Who're we to say it ain't got somethin' goin' for it?"

"Yeah well, they might not feel so cool if they knew the law boys had their number. We need to let Brother Dave know about that, but it don't look like we're gonna get that close to him. Let's talk to Marcos here and maybe he can tell him."

Half an hour later, as dusk fell, the two were escorted back to their hut. "We eat in the mess tent in half an hour and then gather in Brother's for the evening sermon," said Marcos. "I'll see you guys there. Right now I'm going to tell him what you just told me."

As eating time approached, they became aware of scuffled footsteps outside of their shack. Looking out they saw that a line had formed and was shuffling in one direction. They slipped into the queue and moved forward to a large canvas marquee from which extruded aluminium smoke stacks.

Inside, they were handed battered pewter plates and passed down a line of cooks doling out food from steaming containers. The servers were all females, dressed as before in the dowdy costumes of frontierswomen.

Initially, Steve and River had some difficulty in identifying the ingredients – a pool of oatmeal possibly, with a scattering of cabbage leaves and sweet corn on top. The tent was filled with plain collapsible tables with, in the centre of each, a bowl of strawberries.

The diners sat on long benches and ate rapidly in complete silence and then moved away to make room for new arrivals.

Before the friends could choose their spot, Marcos appeared

at their side and steered them towards a table occupied by himself and several others who appeared to be supervising the meal. "Thanks man…" began Steve but he was silenced with a finger to the lips.

"There is a rule of silence. We think of the bounty before us and the wisdom and grace of Brother's mission without which we would be lost," explained Marcos. Steve sneaked a look at River and rolled his eyes theatrically. Nevertheless, they did as they were told and addressed themselves to the food, un-appetising though it looked and, indeed, tasted.

The meal was eaten quickly – five minutes, no more before Marcos summoned them to their feet and led them from the dining tent. The line of people, adults and children, were now heading to the centre; to the leader's white yurt. Once inside, the friends noticed that all began to sit on the ground and, indeed, that most had brought blankets or cushions with them.

Marcos gave them the explanation. "You guys need to find a spot and make yourselves comfortable. If the spirit takes Brother, his addresses can take an hour or two. S'bin known to talk for four hours or more on occasion."

This was not to be such an occasion. When everyone was settled, Brother appeared from the side, accompanied by two handmaidens, one with a pitcher of water and the other with the inevitable bowl of strawberries. He preceded his speech with a ritual now becoming familiar to the visitors. He picked up a handful of strawberries, inhaled deeply and then, putting them down again, dismissed the bearer theatrically. Next he took a deep draft from the pitcher and the carrier stood to one side, ready to ease his throat, no doubt, should the sermon be a long one. As this was happening the crowd became animated and cries of approval and adulation punctuated the silence.

"Thank you Brother."

"Bless you Brother."

"Show us the way Brother."

The leader raised his hand and quiet fell as he began to speak: "Brothers, sisters, children. We meet here today as every day, a family united in love, a community united in spirit. We show the watching world what it is to reject the sensuality and temptation that the benighted are prey to and how we can build instead a strength and resolve that takes us to the edge, the very edge of enlightenment. The world watches but does not understand. We have come far, very far along this road, too far for the watchers to see. We have left them behind.

"I have told you often that when we come to the place at the end of that road, the time of restraint, the time of denial will be over. We will step into a new reality where pleasure and joy will be ours, will have been earned. There will be colour and music, unbounded love and, yes, we will partake at last of the fruit hitherto forbidden.

"I want to tell you now that that time is here. I have learned things today that lead me to the conclusion that the time is now. Tomorrow you must return here at the sun's zenith and we will all journey together to the next phase. Tell the children tonight that they must not be afraid. Tell the children that there will be treats for them tomorrow and that I love them and you all."

Throughout the speech, the audience continued to call out, some singing softly and many weeping openly.

"Take us there Brother," came the cry.

"Lead us Brother."

Such was the level of feeling that some of the children did indeed become alarmed and clung, weeping, to their mothers.

"Lower your emotions brothers and sisters. Don't alarm the children. Children be comforted, this is a happy time. All will be well. Tomorrow at noon. Everyone be here. Sleep in sublime peace tonight. All is well. Our time is come."

With that he and his attendant disappeared back to the side and out of view.

The night was a long one. The trek and the later events of their day had left River and Steve with the expectation of sinking into their beds and sleeping long and well. The palliasses, though, were filled with unevenly distributed and compacted straw which, to make matters worse, was damp and reeked of mould. They had expected silence but surrounding them were frequent murmurings of adult voices and the crying of children that seemed to pass from one to another within their hearing. The temperature had dropped considerably during the night and sleep, such as it was, occurred in only a few hours before the dawn.

They were shaken awake by Marcos, who informed them that the breakfast line was already forming and that they should take advantage on this 'day of days'.

As before, they took their places and shuffled their way to the mess tent. Breakfast made the previous night's meal seem like a gourmet feast – it consisted of a large pool of congealed oatmeal, grey in colour and totally without sweeteners or flavouring. Ravenous by now, the men surprised themselves by the alacrity with which they devoured the mush.

After breakfast, Marcos again took charge of their itinerary and took them to parts of the settlement that they had not yet visited. What they saw was a transformation. They had expected an exodus of able adults to the fields with just older people and children remaining behind for the day. Instead it felt like a holiday. The skies were clear and the sun warm, encouraging people to sit with family or in wider groups outside of their dwellings as though enjoying a community picnic. Many had adorned themselves with colourful pieces of clothing and picked flowers.There were religious overtones, with snatches of hymn-like songs and shouts of exaltation.

As the sun climbed higher in the sky, the atmosphere became increasingly animated and the brothers, sisters and children rose to their feet and began to move, as in a street parade, towards the centre, towards Brother's compound.

Inside Brother's yurt, there was none of the relatively controlled scene that had been apparent the night before. The singing and hand-clapping rose in volume and several individuals rotated around with hands held aloft, eyes staring as though in a trance. Many of the children looked on in astonishment at this, a sight they would not have seen before in their young lives.

The leaders had foreseen the acoustical problems and on the central dais a microphone had been set up. River nudged his companion and drew his attention to the half dozen or so sizeable speakers positioned around the circumference of the yurt. He was surprised at the incursion of such technology into what had, hitherto, seemed a notably rustic setting.

At noon precisely, Brother appeared, once more from the wings, accompanied this time by six men and six women all dressed in white and each holding aloft silver bowls of strawberries. The familiar cries of gratitude and devotion rang out and he raised his hands, palms outstretched until the noise abated sufficiently for him to begin his speech to the faithful.

"Brothers, sisters, children. Here we are, together, united in our faith and love. I see it there before me, in your eyes, in your gentle faces – the love that you have for each other and the love you have for me. The vibe is so strong – I can feel it – I can taste it." As he spoke he reached for the nearest dish and picked up a single strawberry and, holding it in the palm of his hand, stared at it for a full minute before replacing it. There were murmured responses from the gathering.

"Right on brother."

"We feel it , we feel it."

He raised his hand again to hush them before continuing: "You know I've always tried my best for you. God knows it's all been for you. We've tried to live right, to live pure, on a higher plane if you will. But I have to say to you, I must tell you, that it has failed."

"No brother, no," came from someone and was greeted with a round of applause.

Brother raised his hand again, this time in acknowledgement of the protesting voice.

"Not you, not me – we know the right path, we have seen the way. I have shown you the way. So what is the failure? I will tell you. We are before our time. The world is not ready for us and will not follow our example. Greed, excess, venality stalk the land. Dog eat dog – each man against his brother. We have passed through that, come to a different place, but they will not let us be. We are an affront to them. They cannot allow us to survive."

"Fuck 'em," came another response.

"No brother," replied the leader, "The little children are here. Mind the children. Don't upset the children. The forces of darkness lie without. They are here, make no mistake. We must stay calm for the children's sake. Soon the time will be here, it is upon us. Soon we will be able to feast on that which we have long resisted, to be together as those who would destroy us gather in the shadows. They want to take our children from us. We must deal with this in our own way – take responsibility for our own fate. We cannot put our lives in the hands of such primitive and unenlightened people. We have shown the way and they have not followed. Now we must journey on."

"What the fuck's he talkin' about?" whispered Steve to his friend,. his voice betraying his anxiety.

"Sounds like they're gonna let it all hang out with them strawberries any time soon," replied River.

" 'bout time too if you ask me. They could do with a bit of lightnin' up after all this denial crap. Still I'm outa here. If half of what he says is true, it ain't gonna be pretty round here. Cain't see it happening though. Who gives a fuck 'bout a bunch of heads this far outa town."

"You're right," replied River "I've had enough of all this sanctimonious crap too, but getting' clear ain't gonna be easy. You remember what he said about permission to come in and permission to leave and have you seen the goons they got on the gates? Heavy ain't the word man."

The two of them stepped away from the back of a crowd that had become highly emotional. Many voices were raised in song and the bowls of sacred strawberries had been taken from the alcoves and were being paraded aloft by Brother's wives. Hands were raised in supplication as they passed by. The heightened atmosphere continued to affect some of the children who, alarmed by the turn of events, clung to their parents in distress.

"Lower your emotions," Brother continued in an attempt to redeem the situation, "Don't upset the children. It's alright children. There is no pain, we have come this far and it is but a short distance to go. You will be happy. We will *all* be happy. Look upon the strawberries – are they not beautiful? How often have you wanted to eat one? I always told you the day would come. I have never lied to you. I have never lied. Soon, soon we will feast – we will do this together."

As he went on, Steve and River backed off in stages to the yurt's entrance but once gaining it found it blocked by Marco and another guard. The friends looked at each other, unsure what to do next.

Fortune took a hand. Ever since their arrival, their exotic appearance had made it difficult for the younger occupants of the commune to resist staring at them. Two girls in their mid-teens were no exception. As Brother spoke again of strawberries, Steve, ever the joker, mimed eating a handful of them and licked his lips, pantomiming gross enjoyment. The girls clutched at each other, giggling, but their response had been witnessed by the two guards who approached them, leant to whisper in their ears and ushered them back into the crowd.

Steve and River took their chance and slipped out through the tent flap and into the open.

Instinctively they knew there was no time to pick up their packs and they half ran to the perimeter of the settlement only to find the gateway blocked again by two guards, who, although affecting a languid hippie pose, were clearly keeping them under strict observation.

Steve and River slowed down and kicked dust aimlessly as they sauntered over to the gate. They laughed together as though sharing a pleasantry. "Hey man, how's it going?" Steve asked of the first.

"Cool man," came the reply. "Whats'up? You off somewhere? Everyone gotta be with Brother. They're the orders."

"Yeah, we know. Because we ain't part of the family, Brother asked us to scout down the trail apiece to see if any interlopers are approaching."

The two guards raised eyebrows at each other, not sure what to do.

"Tell you what," said River. "We'll take a quick look see and be back in ten." The guards could see for themselves that the two men didn't have their rucksacks with them and, seeming reassured, stepped aside.

Steve and River sauntered casually down the path until they came to the edge of the forest about 100 metres from the settlement. River started to push on, unprepared for Steve's next action. He had turned back towards the guards, who were watching intently from a distance. Reaching into his shoulder bag, he lifted out a handful of strawberries and crushed them to his face before swallowing a big mouthful. Then he flipped the bird with both red-stained hands.

River jumped in alarm. "For fuck's sake man, what the fuck are you…"

But the guards had begun scurrying towards them. The two turned as one and began to run towards the forest path. River had a look of fear on his face, but Steve seemed to have gone crazy. As they ran he whooped in exhilaration, throwing more one-fingered salutes over his shoulders.

Soon they come to the fork in the path. They knew now that the right branch would take them to the clearing with the strawberry plantations and the left back, eventually, to the safety of Boulder Creek. Taking the left, they ran on for another ten minutes before stopping for a while to listen. The forest was silent.

Steve reached again into his shoulder bag and hoicked out another handful of berries. "Here man, take some – you deserve it."

River, shocked and ashen faced, shook his head. "Why d'you do that? We were out of there… we were cool."

Steve grinned at him, his face smeared with red juice, looking as fierce as a painted warrior. "Just because man. They were so fuckin' up themselves – so sure they were right about everything. I mean, all that sacred strawberry crap. Most of them looked half dead. What the fuck're they afraid of? A bit of fruit in their diet? Would've worked wonders. So what if it got their juices runnin'?. S'what life's all about ain't it. Fuck 'em." And with that he pushed another handful of berries into his mouth.

After another half hour on the trail, they felt certain that no one was following. River had gradually pulled ahead of Steve and was the first to come to the stream. He knelt down to fill his water bottle, expecting Steve to do likewise. But when Steve caught up, he slumped down on a boulder, clutching his gut. "Hey, I don't feel so good. I mean it hurts man."

"Maybe you ate too many berries," said River.

"It ain't like that. This is somethin' else – it fuckin' hurts."

River was shocked now to look at him. Steve's face was a waxy white and the contrast with the earlier staining gave him the look, less now of a warrior, and more that of a grotesque clown. There were thick beads of sweat on his forehead, but despite that he was shivering, if not shaking.

"Here, take a drink." He handed his bottle to his friend, who took it but made no attempt to lift it to his lips. River guided his hand and tipped the bottle but most of the liquid spilled down Steve's juice-stained chin.

"I need to rest man," mumbled Steve. "Just need to lie down for ten. I'll be cool."

River listened again to the forest and found it still to be silent, but he was apprehensive, not sure they had put enough distance between themselves and the Strawberry people.

"Okay man, he said. "You do that. I'm gonna go back down the trail awhile, make sure ain't no one followin'."

Steve lowered himself laboriously to the ground and lay back on the moss. River removed his jacket before leaving and placed it gently over his friend. "Be back soon man," he said.

He jogged back along the trail, pausing each minute to listen. There was nothing to hear apart from birdcalls and even they were infrequent. Nothing was disturbing the path behind them. Satisfied, he turned back down the trail.

Everything was as he had left it at the stream. Steve had

made no move and had his eyes closed. Reluctant as River was to wake him, he was anxious to move on. Although it was still just mid-afternoon, he thought they should get back to the town well before sundown. They would need to restock and then find a way out of there with one of the passing truck drivers. He thought he could give Steve another five minutes but no more.

The time up, he went to wake his friend. Christ, he thought, he looks worse than when I left him. A vigorous shaking brought no response and it was then that he noticed the foam that had collected around Steve's lips, which were the colour of ox tongue.

For a minute or two, he stood looking at the rushing stream, not sure what to do. His mind was a blank. It was as though all of their camaraderie, the situation they were in – everything – had drained away in a moment and nothing had replaced it. And then thoughts did rush in – the options.

There was nothing he could do about Steve in his condition; he couldn't carry him and he was reluctant to leave him alone in *their* territory. He needed to find help fast.

His mind made up and pausing only to draw his jacket back over Steve, he turned back on to the trail, running now in his anxiety. It took a further half-hour to get the edge of the forest and the single track road that he knew led back to the town. As he broke clear, he came to a stop, shocked by the sight before him.

The road was littered with police patrol cars and other off-road vehicles. There were policemen but others too – state troopers he guessed – maybe thirty or so individuals, most of them armed. Indeed, some were checking their weapons as he looked on.

He had taken them by surprise but once they spotted him they moved fast enough. Weapons were pointed in his direction and instructions barked at him. "On the ground, on the ground now. Goddamn it, on the ground arsehole!"

He did as he was told and offered no resistance as his hands were cuffed behind him. Then he attempted to talk to his assailants. "My friend – you must help me – in the woods. He's sick, very sick, he ..."

The response was a kick in the ribs.

"Shut the fuck up. You one o' them strawberry boys ain't you – back up the trail apiece?"

"No, please, I ..."

"I said shut it motherfucker." Another kick came and River had little choice but to remain silent. The man who kicked him seemed to be in charge and now shouted at those around him: "Seems they know we comin' guys. This here piece of shit been sent to parley."

He knelt down and dropping his voice, spoke quickly to River. "Here's the deal fella. OK so you got a friend ain't so good. We got a medic with us. You show us the trail back to the strawberry people and we'll fix your friend."

River was allowed to his feet, and still hand-cuffed was pushed back down the path with the troopers following. The commander bellowed his instructions. "You know your orders – move in swift, move in tight. There're women and children there, so no unnecessary rough stuff. Cain't speak for the guys though! The land ain't theirs to shit on so we just movin' them on, movin' them on. Go, go, go."

When they reached the stream, there was no sign of Steve

in the place where River had left him.

"You shittin' us boy – ain't no one here – this some kinda trap?" sneered the commander. He instructed his men to look around and it wasn't long before there was a call from further down the stream.

"Over here captain, we got him." It was then that River noticed the drag trail from where he had left his friend.

Steve had crawled to the water's edge, presumably to drink. He was on his back which was arched. His hands were held out in front of him, clawed. The eyes, clouded white-skinned globes, were wide open. But none of these things were what held the gaze of the troopers and reduced them to silence. The face, contorted in pain, was ivory white, the teeth bared and the mouth painted with gashes of vibrant red. There was, otherwise, no sign of life.

"Shee-it," said the commander. "We got ourselves a situation here. Ain't nothing we can do for this dude, gotta be on our toes now – ain't no tellin' what we gonna be up against. We'll pick him up on the way back."

River had fallen to his knees in shock and grief and when the commander tried to get him to stand, he was unable to do so. All strength had drained from his limbs. He was grabbed painfully by his hair and his head was yanked back. "Which way now fella?"

River mumbled his reply as if in a dream. "Stay on the path, take the right fork."

The commander turned to one of his men and ordered him to stay with the two friends, one now dead and one incapacitated with shock. Then he yelled to the rest, "Ok let's move it. We real close now. Let's go."

Lying face down in the dirt, River, in that moment, understood something for the first time. Lifting his head, he screamed out his warning. "No, stop, listen to me, strawberries...the strawberries...you don't get it...please..."

The minder grabbed him again by his hair and pushed his face back into the ground. He choked and spluttered, his mouth filling with soil and leaves, as the troopers raced on down the trail and out of earshot.